Walking Wounded

All the very best,

Anna

Dedication

To my husband Neil, and my children, Thomas and Emma, always my best fans. Thank you all for your patience, support and understanding, and for sleeping late during those holidays while I sat and typed outside in the early morning sunshine. Now, and only now, are you allowed to read on...

Walking Wounded

Anna Franklin Osborne

GooseWing Publications

British Library Cataloguing in Publication Data
A catalogue record for this book is available from the British Library

ISBN 978-09935690-0-5

Typeset by Amolibros, Milverton, Somerset
www.amolibros.co.uk
This book production has been managed by Amolibros
Printed and bound by Lightning Source

Anna Osborne (nee Franklin) lives in a village in The New Forest with her husband, two children and ever-increasing menagerie of animals, where she practises as a chiropractor in the local GP surgery as well as teaching at the Anglo-European College of Chiropractic. Over the past five years she has increasingly explored her long-held desires to write and to sing; and as well as singing with the Chicken Soup Choir, she has written a number of short stories. *Walking Wounded* is her first novel, inspired by the lives of her grandmother and her Great Auntie Lil and catalysed by walking on the D-Day beaches telling her children about her great-uncles who were part of that Longest Day.

Acknowledgements

To Rien Doorn, with many, many thanks for the beautiful illustration inspired by reading an early copy of *Walking Wounded*.

Part One

1918, Mons, Belgium, 5 a.m.

He awoke with a shock as an icy rivulet of water finally penetrated the gap between his collar and his neck and trickled down inside his sodden greatcoat.

With a sigh, Sergeant Edward Peters leant back against the boards, squinting up with resignation into the rain dripping endlessly into the deep trench. The rain had woken him from a fitful sleep, punctuated by the sound of snores from his fellow soldiers, the occasional muffled curse. He shifted his long frame uncomfortably, and shuddered with disgust as he felt a rat scuttle across his legs and drop into the stinking mud next to him. No matter how many trenches he dug, how many wounds he patched up, how much blood he saw, he reflected grimly, he would never get used to the rats. He vowed to himself silently that he would never tolerate one in the house again when he got back home to London, that he would fill the house with cats and wage his own tiny and very personal war against the rodents which had plagued his life for the past four years.

He smiled as he thought how much Edie would love that. She loved animals but couldn't have any in the crowded house she lived in in Muswell Hill, but, one day, he thought firmly, one day, they would start afresh and fill their own home with pets and children. He fumbled in the pocket of his greatcoat then, trying to extricate something with his clumsy fingers, numbed with cold. Finally, his fingers alighted on the little photo, and he sat drinking in the sight of his girl, smiling shyly at him all those miles away but so close he could feel her.

His eyes filled with tears suddenly, and he had to catch his breath in that bitter November morning to steady himself.

Then the captain stirred and stumbled out of his shack at the end of the trench.

'Time to be up, lads,' he said quietly passing along the line of men still sleeping in the bottom of the trench, just inches from the foul mud, 'time to get ready.'

Edward gazed one last time at the picture in his hand, then stuffed it carefully back into his pocket. He blew on his hands and caught the captain's eye, nodded grimly at what he saw there.

At 6 a.m. he blew the whistle.

1918 London 11 a.m.

Florence Johnson stood stiffly to attention, clutching the hand of her eldest daughter, Edie, as she listened to the bells pealing out the Armistice on that cold, wintry morning.

As the sound of the last chime died away, it seemed that all of London erupted at last into cheers, the sounds of laughter and joy mingling with the echoes of the great bells. Feeling disorientated and utterly disconnected with the crowd surging around them, Florence half-turned towards Edie, immediately saw the tears running down her cheeks and pulled her close, hugging her tightly. The eldest of her children, barely twenty but old beyond her years, Edie had grown up so much during this seemingly endless war, and with both of them bereft of their menfolk they had become more like sisters as they leaned on each other's quiet strength to look after the family together.

'So what happens now, Mum?' Edie asked distantly, like Florence, removed from the jostle and raucous noise surrounding them.

Florence let out the breath she realised she had been holding with a sigh, hugging her close as if she were still a child.

'We wait for them to come home, love,' she replied, 'then we can start looking after them again.'

In the confusion and euphoria of the next few days and weeks, the troops began to arrive home, spilling out of ferries and trains in a long, exhausted line. They were met with tears and laughter, by women who loved them and children who barely knew them. Their exuberance, their noise and boisterous jokes were a thin veneer over the pain and sadness etched on their young faces, and for many, as soon as they were away from the camaraderie of their units, that veneer would begin to crack under the strain.

Florence and Edie had to endure another two weeks before their men came home. William came first, arriving at the station from where he had left, where Florence had stood desperately swallowing back her treacherous tears four long, painful years before.

As she stood on the platform, trying hard not to allow herself to glance at the clock again, Florence let her mind wander back to that day, and the days just before when her husband first told her he was volunteering to fight.

Oh, she had been so angry with William when he'd signed up, and yet so proud! He had gone alone to do it, then came straight home afterwards with a face so full of emotion she had known what he'd done before he'd spoken. She remembered sadly how she had wept then, and railed at him, her rage that he could do this without consulting her bubbling over. The children, just Edie, Reggie, and Bert in those days, sat frozen with fear, staring at her with shocked eyes; they had never seen her lose her temper, she rarely even raised her voice to them, and never, ever, her hand.

Eventually, William stopped her protests and torrent of fury simply, with a hard hug and a kiss. Then pulled away from her and looked at her directly, and she saw the iron determination written in his face, her heart sinking as she recognised the depth of his commitment.

'You know I have to do this, you know we all do.'

And that was that. No more discussion, his fate and hers sealed with his signature on a scrap of paper, taken the King's shilling like so many men before him. And yet that night, despite her anger and her fear, her pride for him came through and she welcomed him to bed with open arms and forgave him with her loving body.

Florence smiled fondly at her memories then; she had known immediately that she was pregnant again, in fact she had prayed she was, as she waved him off that hot morning in July. That was Lydia, her beautiful but tough little daughter, and carrying her had helped distract her from the news from the Front, had kept her occupied with the relentless business of caring for and feeding a newborn as well as keeping the house going for the older children.

William had only seen Lydia once, she thought sadly, a twinge of apprehension gripping her heart, and he may not even know about the life blossoming within her, and suddenly she spread her hands protectively over her swollen stomach, unconsciously mimicking the actions of four years ago when she had seen him off to war. She wasn't sure if any of her letters had got to him in the past few months, she had heard nothing and she doubted suddenly if he even knew of this baby's existence. This pregnancy had been another precious gift, another blessing borne of passion for her brave, exhausted husband who had come home on leave earlier this year and loved her as if he feared he would never see her again.

He had missed so much, she realised suddenly, had been away so long, and her heart began to race in panic that they might never fill the gaps between them. That he would never feel her despair when she had sat up, night after night, spooning boiled beef broth into little Lydia when her milk dried up, too poor to afford a wet-nurse and with no one to ask for advice. That he would never understand her pride that, despite the endless miscarriages – she closed her eyes sharply to block those memories – she had borne four children and lost none.

And all of a sudden, the waiting was over. As she opened her eyes, Florence saw him stepping down from the train, her daydream and reality meeting with a discordant clash. Her husband, her William, so familiar yet hauntingly different, walking haltingly along the platform with his eyes fixed on hers, his eyes fixed upon a vision from another world, another lifetime.

Florence felt her heart pounding in her chest, knew she had just the fraction of a moment to make everything all right.

'Hello, love,' she said, looking steadily at him, bravely tilting her chin up to meet his gaze, hoping desperately that it would be enough to make it as it should be.

And wordlessly, he opened his arms and swept her up in them, clutching her to him as though his life depended on it. Florence was horrified to feel the lack of substance to him, the frailty of a man who had been pushed too far for too long, and pulled herself away to look him in the eye, appalled to note the yellow pallor of the whites as she did so. He backed away then, shaking his head defensively.

'Don't ask me about it, Florence. Don't ever, ever ask me.'

And as they turned to leave the platform, Florence felt a cold dread threatening to engulf her aching heart, as icy and chilling as the London fog swirling about them as their feet marked the well-worn but suddenly unfamiliar path for home. And walking without touching, she understood with bitter clarity that this shocking silence was to envelop and separate them, like so many others of their time, for the rest of their lives.

Edie had to wait another six hours, but with the resilience that had seen her through the past four years, she simply took a deep breath and endured it. She smiled at her mother, confused and wondering at the strain on her face when Florence had hoped and prayed for so long for William to come home. Sitting in the cosy warmth of the kitchen, she forced herself to play with little Lydia, filled that interminable day trying to talk to her dad, and trying to help Mum connect with this stranger in their midst. To begin with, Lydia was shy of the grey-faced man at the kitchen table, but soon her inquisitive and irrepressible nature took over and she climbed boldly up onto his lap giggling as she always did, clutching at his moustache with chubby little hands, her black curls raising a weary, delighted smile from William as he slowly, unbelievingly contemplated the new addition to his family. Then eventually the news of their father's return must have spread through the street, and shutting up shop early the boys hurtled through the kitchen door, Reg enthusiastically pumping his dad's hand while his more reserved younger brother, Bert, stood grinning shyly, then daringly suggesting a pint at their local pub which he had been too young to frequent when he had last seen him.

'That'll probably do him more good than anything,' sighed Florence tiredly, as they left, pushing her hair away from her face. She felt exhausted from the emotional turmoil of the day, the conflict of emotions from what she remembered of her husband she loved and the new reality of the unfamiliar, broken man who had come back to her, bearing the scars of mustard gas and much, much more besides. She looked at Edie then, and her heart went out to her, the poor girl had been so brave all day waiting for news of Edward, yet she hadn't said a word about it, had swallowed her own anxieties and fears so as not to detract from her family's joy on her father's return.

'Why don't you go and ask his mum if she's had any word?' she suggested sympathetically, but just as the words left her mouth, there was a knock on the back door.

Edie felt her heart miss a beat and froze, looking at her mother helplessly, her trepidation suddenly rendering her both speechless and immobile. Florence smiled at her tenderly, then straightened her apron and marched to the door, flinging it open determinedly.

And in came Edward. Still in uniform, exhausted and grimy, a broad smile across his face and his arms open wide. Edie gazed at him, feeling a wave of emotion flooding through her body and threatening to swamp her, then fell into them, laughing and crying, trying to reach her arms around the bulk of him in his jacket. Then to her surprise, he let go abruptly and looked at her for a long time, drinking in the sight of the woman whose memory had kept him going during the bleak days and nights in the trenches.

Then he sank down on one knee on the scrubbed kitchen floor, took her hand between his, and said in a voice hoarse with emotion,

'Edith Rose Johnson, will you marry me?'

The next few days passed in a blur. The excitement of the war ending, the boys coming home, and now Edie's engagement all had a dreamlike quality, and Florence felt her way through them carefully, knowing that a gulf existed between her and her husband that she had yet to navigate.

On the surface, he was the same old William, a carbon copy of Reggie and Bert, although his black hair now had a stubborn white streak at his temple. He seemed at peace in the daytime, loving nothing more than pulling the now doting Lydia up onto his lap and singing to her in his soft voice. But as the day wore on, he would become increasingly agitated and tense, avoiding his wife's eye as she worked around him in the house. And each night, when the boys got back from working in the shop, he would leap up with barely disguised relief and suggest he took them out for a pint, leaving with a backward guilty glance and arriving home too late and too drunk to talk, falling into bed and sleeping within moments.

And then one night, the nightmares started. It was a Tuesday, stocktaking day for the boys, so Florence was not expecting them home until late as they would usually meet their friends at the pub directly after finishing work. She has arranged for Edie to take Lydia out for a play with friends, her daughter looking at her with sudden, bashful understanding, 'I'll buy her fish and chips and have an early night, Mum.'

She glanced ruefully at herself in the mirror, a little embarrassed that she was feeling shy because of what she had planned, then pulled the pretty fabric of her favourite maternity smock down over her neat but expanding bump and walked downstairs with a determined smile pinned on her face. William barely looked up as she entered the kitchen and for a moment she hesitated. She felt the fear of rejection deep within her, threatening to let her down, and she almost, almost faltered. But then the courage that had never failed her yet led her three paces further to cross the divide to the man she loved, and with heartfelt relief she felt the familiar desire stirring for the man sitting before her taking over, and she bent to kiss him full on the lips, feeling his startled but then enthusiastic response.

William broke away and looked at her, smiling, but Florence was in no mood to talk. Needing to find this moment, this intimacy with her husband, she took his hand and led him upstairs, feeling the warmth flood through her as he slid into bed and covered her body with his own.

Much later, they rolled away from one another, but fell asleep still touching, neither aware that each slept with a gentle smile on their face.

Many hours later, Florence awoke with a shock. Her first thought was that Lydia must be ill, strange cries calling to her maternal instinct and forcing her from blissful sleep, and she sat up disorientated, realising with her waking breath that the cries came from William, her husband. Shakily, she reached out and touched him, seeing that he was still asleep but dreaming, and watched helplessly as he recoiled away from her trembling hand and howled like a lost soul.

The next morning, Florence waited until everyone had left the house, then turned to William, her hands on her hips and a challenge in her eyes that he wanted to avoid, staring silently down at the table and hoping against hope that she would just drop it, leave him alone.

'William,' she tried, tentatively, 'William please tell me what last night was about. Do you remember what you were dreaming of?'

William looked up at her reluctantly, and saw reflected in her loving face what he had most feared to see.

Pity.

Furiously he stood, shook his head as he if were trying to shake away the violence of his thoughts, and without a word, slammed out of the house. Shocked by his reaction, Florence watched him walk away, head bent and shoulders hunched, then felt her knees give way and sank down at the table, finally giving way to the burning tears she had been holding back and weeping at her impotence, stricken to the heart.

The nightmares continued, relentlessly. Florence could see no pattern to them, sometimes they were almost as he first drifted off to sleep, sometimes after a few hours, but the effect was always the same. First the thrashing around, then the crying out, then the shocked, sweat-drenched face of the man she loved, staring glassily into the darkness and unable, or unwilling, she thought bitterly, to tell her what he had seen. He would turn to her then, holding her tight, finding some solace in her nearness and in her body, but never, ever, talking. Not ever.

Edie could sense the gulf between her parents, but thought her brothers seemed to be helping, talking to her dad down at the pub and behaving as if he'd never been away. Now that Dad was back, she found the intimacy that had sprung up during the war years with her mother had been lost, yet she knew instinctively that her mum needed her even though she had no idea how to help.

Not knowing where to turn she began to spend more and more time with Edward, feeling a guilty weight lift from her shoulders each night that they walked out together, leaving the new and unfamiliar tension of the big house behind. Edward had begun to split his time between his home and hers, arriving as soon as he could each evening to take her for a walk, and Florence allowed them to go off alone. After all, she reasoned, the boy had just survived the war to end all wars, surely she could trust him with her eldest daughter?

So each and every evening, Edie and Edward walked and talked, her hand tightly clenched in his and thrust deep into the pocket of his overcoat as they walked through the grounds of Alexandra Palace, his eyes fixed on the distant lights as he bared his soul and told her, word by painful, grating word, about his war. About the blood and the rats, the lice and the endless, stinking mud. Mind-numbing, paralysing fear. She never commented, shocked by the raw pain in his voice as he told her of the atrocities he'd seen, the conditions he'd suffered. She had no idea what to say, so unwittingly she did the best thing she could possibly have done to help him heal, she just listened, tears running down her face unchecked, and held his hand while he talked.

They set a date. 'As soon as possible,' Edward declared, I've waited long enough!'

They were sitting in the front room of the big house on Muswell Hill to mark the occasion, the unused fire stoked up for the first time in years. Lydia had been sent, protesting, to bed, but Reggie, Bert and the whole family were all here to discuss the wedding plans.

'I really can't fix anything too soon,' protested Florence weakly, 'we can't throw a party with what we've got, let alone a wedding!' She glanced across the room to William for support, but he looked away, refusing to catch her eye. She sighed, knowing that he would not engage in this little family drama, nor any other battle she needed him to fight for her again.

Edie straightened her back and looked at her mother and father earnestly.

'Mum, listen to me,' she urged, gently. 'Edward and I have already waited too long! I'm twenty now, and quite able to make my own decisions. We want to get married soon, we can fix it ourselves, just our family and Edward's mum. We don't need a big do, but we really want to get married next month, Mum.' She sat back breathlessly and stared down at the pattern on the rug, her piece said and painfully aware of her heart thumping in her chest as she waited for a verdict.

'But what will you wear?' wailed Florence plaintively, aware of how silly she sounded but nonetheless clutching at straws, not ready for any more change in her world, and certainly not ready for her eldest to fly the nest and leave her to cope.

Edie relaxed and laughed out loud, smiling with relief at Edward who had broken out into a huge grin.

'I can still fit into my green dress you made me, Mum,' she insisted, 'and I've always loved it.'

Florence looked at her, horror-struck, a phrase from her own mother, from her own chaotic childhood clamouring in her mind, then springing unbidden to her lips, 'But you can't wear green for a wedding, it's bad luck!'

Edie laughed again and Edward joined in this time.

'Mrs Johnson,' he said quietly, 'we've just come through the biggest war this world has ever seen. It's time we made our own luck, don't you think?'

The date was set for mid-December, barely a month after Edward and William had come home. Edie danced through those days, feeling that her heart might just burst with happiness as she scribbled lists and made plans, pooh-poohing any obstacle that presented itself. Each morning she smiled to herself as her eyes fell on the dress hanging on the back of her door, elegant and grown-up, especially with the creamy lace wrap Florence had tearfully lent her to go with it with the cold drawing in now as winter came with a vengeance to North London.

But unbeknown to them all, a new enemy was sweeping across Europe, as deadly as the Germans, but this time silent and unseen.

Florence was the first to get sick. The 'flu' that year was particularly virulent, although no one yet knew what a toll it was to take, on a world already weakened by wartime nutrition, grief and exhaustion. She woke one morning with a banging pain in her head, and feverish and confused; Florence took to her bed for the first time in the family's memory, even for childbirth she had never been out of the picture for more than a day at a time. Now, she lay in the dark for days on end and coughed painfully, recovering slowly as her beloved Edie nursed her gently and kindly though the worst with cooling flannels and nourishing beef broth.

Then Edie was next. She awoke one morning with pain in her neck, alarmed at the size of the swollen glands she could feel there.

'Mum,' she called out in distress, and taking one practised look at her, Florence pushed her gently back down onto the bed, put a cold flannel on her forehead just like Edie had done for her, and settled her down to sleep. When the fever kicked in, Edie lost track of time. Lost track of whole days as worried faces swam in and out of her vision, mainly her mother, who made everybody else stay away, reasoning that she and she alone should be in contact with Edie.

But unlike her mother, Edie did not have the resistance borne of age. Her weakened frame grew thinner and more frail, and over the next few days, instead of rallying as her mother had done, her lucid moments grew fewer.

'How is she?' demanded William gruffly, as Florence left the room that afternoon; he had been told to stay away but was desperate for news, feeling utterly out of depth in the face of his daughter's illness and his wife's fatigue.

'She's peaceful,' said Florence, then felt a sob welling up inside her, catching in her throat and threatening to choke her. Struggling to control herself but failing in her exhaustion and despair, she burst out,

'I don't know, I don't know, oh God, I don't know! She seems so weak, our baby girl, William, how can this be happening?'

The enormity of her fear for her daughter and her helplessness in the face of this terrible illness overwhelmed her then, and weeping finally, she fell into his arms. And for the first time since his return, William rose to the occasion, putting his own misery aside to comfort her, stroking her hair back from her brow, pallid with exhaustion and despair. All they could do now was hold each other and wait.

Much later that day, Edie lay in the darkened room, suddenly becoming awake and aware. Someone was in there with her, she could feel it. Painfully, she turned her head to the side – and there, there she saw him, her Edward, smiling at her and holding out his hands just like he had when he had returned from the Front. Gladly, she reached her hands out to him and felt a wave of relief as the most overwhelming peace enveloped her body.

When Florence entered the room again that afternoon, she knew she was gone before she touched her. She stood silently, knowing that Edie's presence, her energy, had left the room, leaving a still husk on the bed, a memory of what might have been. Numbly, Florence went and sat on the bed and looked at her first-borne for a long time, quietly stroking her peaceful face, which seemed to her to hold the remains of a smile. Then like a dam breaking, wept the first of a river of tears.

Edie was buried in her green dress. Florence had torn it down at first, hell-bent on an orgy of destruction, her mother's own ghost tormenting her that the dress was to blame. It was Edward that saved her from those demons, holding her and weeping on the day of the funeral, finally letting his own feelings out in a flood of bitter tears.

'It was never the dress,' he managed finally. 'It was never the dress. It made her so happy to be wearing something you made her, you know she always loved what you made. It was just the flu, no rhyme and no reason, and you know that really, Mrs Johnson.'

She drew back and laughed harshly.

'For pity's sake, after all we've been through, call me Florence,' she gulped. 'I know you're right, but Edward, it just seems so unfair. She waited for you all these years and you came through without a wound, I just wanted you both to have your share of happiness now.'

She stopped abruptly, unable to go on, desperately trying to contain her own grief as she was forced to acknowledge the end of a dream in the destroyed face of the young man before her. Edward dropped his face into his hands.

'She kept me going, you know,' he said quietly. 'If it hadn't been for her, I don't think I could have gone on out there. I had an image of her in my mind all the time, and every time it got too much, she was there for me, helping me block out what I could see and what I had to do.'

Florence looked at him sadly, unaware of the tears streaming down her face.

'Was it bad, love?' she asked, tenderly, reaching out to him with the question she had been forbidden to ask her husband but had been longing to ask him ever since he first stepped down from the train.

He nodded, mutely, staring at her, realising suddenly that William hadn't told her anything, any of it. Understanding finally just what a gift Edie had given him, just allowing him to walk and talk. Allowing him time to heal.

He reached out and held her. Then, in a silent ritual of love and grief, they dressed Edie together and followed her coffin out into the rain.

In the midst of grief, new life was born.

One chilly January morning of 1919, just a few short weeks after Edie had died, Florence woke to the familiar, gripping pains of early labour.

Holding her breath, she eased herself up carefully, moving quietly so as not to awaken William sleeping deeply at her side. For a little while she sat on the edge of the bed, feeling the gripping surge of power gathering in her abdomen, her hands pressed firmly against her nightie and calmly counting and timing the contractions. Soon she padded softly out of the door, put the kettle on the hob to boil and meticulously washed herself at the kitchen sink, aware of the utter silence of the slumbering household all around her. All of a sudden, she gasped as a much stronger contraction swept over her, making her double over and grip the sink to help her pant through the pain.

'Are you all right, love?'

Florence jumped, startled by the sudden voice behind her, and turned to see William's concerned face as he strode across the kitchen and wrapped his arms around her straining body. She leaned against him with relief, a little rush of joy that he had sensed her need for him without her calling for help flooding through her.

'I'm fine,' she answered, uncertainly, then cried out again as another contraction hit her, William holding her steady as she clenched her hands in his. 'It just seems to be building up a bit quickly, that's all.'

Then pain overtook her and she lost track of time, turning her focus to the storm within, barely aware of the flurry of activity around her – Reggie rushing off under marching orders from his dad to fetch the midwife, Bert leaving with Lydia's hand clutched in his, both faces looking equally young and frightened as they scurried past their mother to get out of the door.

Then the feeling of exultation as she began to push, her determination finally overriding the pain. And when Florence heard the tiny cry with a rush of relief and a surge of love, she raised her head to look at the midwife with the age-old question on her lip, 'Is it all right?'

The midwife smiled sympathetically and nodded, 'A beautiful boy.'

Florence smiled exhaustedly and let her head fall back for a moment, then her eyes jerked open in alarm as yet another wave of pain hit her.

'Shhh, shhh, it's just the afterbirth, one more push, you're nearly done,' soothed the midwife, but Florence shook her head wildly, heaved herself up on her elbows, and pushed again, a wail of pain hissing between her clenched teeth.

And so another little life came unexpectedly and miraculously into the world, little May following hard on the heels of her twin brother, Stanley, two babies to fill the hearts and minds of the little family still reeling from the loss of the eldest. Two babies, black curls and chubby fists waving, awakening in their sister Lydia her first taste of maternal love, and a new focus and vitality to their still grieving parents.

Two babies to take them forwards, away from the twin tragedy of the war and the family loss they had endured in the aftermath, towards a future they could only hope and pray would be worth all the fighting, all the killing and all the dying.

Part Two

1945, London

The wireless finally crackled and fell silent, the words of Winston Churchill still reverberating in the silence of the room and through the turmoil of May's mind. She couldn't believe her ears. The war in Europe was over, and the boys were coming home, yet all May could do was stare blindly into the fire, twisting her diamond ring endlessly around her finger as she tried to envisage what the news meant to her, what fate now lay in store for her and her little girl.

Tears beginning to choke her throat, May swallowed hard and drew a long, shuddering breath, remembering. Trying to make a decision, to answer a dilemma that she was afraid she would never feel ready to face. She glanced down at her ring, her beautiful face bitter. A cluster of tiny diamonds glinting in the firelight, reflecting memories of that fateful day in 1939 when Jimmy had asked her to marry him, on his knees outside the pub in Muswell Hill.

They had walked through the grounds of Alexandra Palace that evening, the lights of London twinkling as far as they could see and adding to the enchantment of the already frosty night.

She said yes immediately, without thinking. It was to be expected, they had been walking out together for nearly a year. When her sister asked her why, much, much later, she would one day confess it was out of pity, his skinny features pitiful in the chill evening air, so vulnerable and so young.

His love for her was slavish, his courtship passionate. She had been intrigued at first, then embarrassed. But everybody seemed to like him, and on paper, he was just the ticket. A hardworking mechanic, he had already finished his apprenticeship and had his eye on running the little garage where he worked, in fact, his boss Bob had already been heard gruffly admitting how much he needed the youngster.

Yet, even then, May had sensed there was more to Jimmy, and looking back, the older, wiser May shuddered at the naivety of the nineteen-year-old in her mind's eye. Even that girl, that child had sensed that Jimmy had a dark side to him that no one else knew, and could be moody and volatile at times. She had to confess she had found this exciting, his stormy moments always made him appear more passionate, and when they passed, he would immediately be regretful and sweet to her, so sweet. And if she was honest, she had liked the power she seemed to have to excite him and make him jealous and angry and then so sweetly sorry.

May had never had power before. The youngest of the six children (although she could not remember Edie and Stanley had preceded her by barely five minutes), she was still very much the baby of the family, with the fewest responsibilities, the fewest worries, and the least say in anything that mattered. Although she knew that she had it easy in many ways, as she grew older she was beginning to chafe at being dismissed as a baby, being overruled and ignored.

Jimmy's love and her ability to inflame and then calm him felt like a whole new world. She tasted the power every girl feels as she becomes a woman, and she relished the transition.

So when he held out his dead mother's ring on that chilly autumn evening, she had said yes, instinctively and emphatically, sealing her fate without a second thought. She was ready to stretch her wings and fly.

And now, on this dark night so many years later while the rest of the world celebrated the end of another war, who would have thought she would be sitting here, viciously twisting her beautiful ring as if she were trying to wrench it off her roughened and chapped finger to fly again, but this time to fly away?

1939

Stanley paused for a moment, catching his breath after unloading the delivery. The family shop was in his hands today, as it always seemed to be on delivery day, he muttered to himself churlishly, then valiantly did his best to dismiss the uncharacteristic thought from his mind.

He straightened his back wearily and sighed. Soon to be twenty years old, he was well used to the back-breaking labour of stocking the shelves, and was quietly proud of the family's little corner shop, selling everything from sweets and hair ribbons through to buckets of coal. He just sometimes wished his brothers might help him out more, he thought, wryly, but then again, he didn't have to concern himself with the orders and accounts as they would so loftily remind him.

Still, he wouldn't have minded a swift one down the pub tonight, it would have been nice to see Millie if she was serving.

He sighed again. Stanley was a quiet lad, happiest doing his own thing, minding his own business and preferably immersed in a world of parchment and charcoal conjuring up pictures with his gifted, sensitive hands. Lately though, he had begun to feel lonely, especially as little May was forever out with Jimmy, and if she wasn't with him, she was talking about him.

He smiled fondly as he thought of his twin. He wished he could talk to her about Millie as he and May would talk about everything else of importance, always relishing, dissecting and chewing over each other's problems, but then again, there was nothing to talk about, was there, he admitted to himself, ruefully. He had never spoken to her, couldn't muster the courage to do more than order a pint and duck his head down with a mumbled word of thanks.

He grimaced to himself, stretched one final time then started stacking the next shelf.

Millie stood on tiptoe at the bar to see if she could catch a fleeting glimpse of Stanley. One of his brothers had ordered a round earlier, but so far all she could see was a bunch of blokes gathered near the piano with their backs to her. Two jet black-haired men, she was none the wiser, Stanley and his brothers were so alike to look at, that despite the disparity in their ages, she would need him to turn round to be sure.

A moment later, someone opened the piano and began to hammer out a few tinny notes. As everyone began to crowd round, enthusiastically drumming their appreciation with their hands on their thighs, she realised with a wave of disappointment that he wasn't with them tonight.

Probably running the shop alone again, she thought disapprovingly, pursing her lips in irritation. She liked Stanley well enough, but they had yet even to talk. He was too shy, and let's face it, she thought crossly, they were both too busy, her in the pub till all hours, and Stanley in the shop that never seemed to close.

'Oi!!! Penny for your thoughts! A man could die of thirst over here!'

She jumped and turned abruptly, acknowledging with a guilty grin the queue forming at the bar. Pulling herself together and pasting on a bright smile for the next customer, she thrust her little pipe dream of Stanley firmly out of her mind and began to pull the next pint.

Lydia was scrubbing pots and pans in the kitchen sink, cursing her luck. At twenty-four, she should have been married by now, she mused ruefully, but Lydia had always carried her sense of duty as if she had the weight of the world on her shoulders, and raising their orphaned family would always come before her own desires.

She had left school in those desperate days after Mum died, simply walked out of the classroom despite being under age and stepped into her shoes, taking over from her in the shop and running the home. Now that the boys were doing more and more, she hardly seemed to leave the house these days, she thought tiredly, endlessly cooking and cleaning, just like Mum had before her.

She caught her breath sharply when she thought of Mum. Every time the loss still shocked her, the power of it undiminished even after all this time.

She had been ten at the time. If truth be told, she'd suspected Mum had not been well for a long time, although it would be years before Lydia truly understood what had really happened that terrible night. Mum had seemed exhausted, and some mornings she would hear her rushing outside to the privy. Once she saw her coming back inside, and she was ashen, shaky, and Lydia thought she might have just been sick.

The night she died, Lydia had awoken to a commotion, a series of short, gasping screams, then muffled curses from her father, followed by low, harsh weeping which frightened her so much she had not dared leave the bedroom she shared with the twins to investigate.

She saw the mattress being taken out the next morning. Dad had been trying to bundle it out in a hurry, but her sharp eyes had already noted the dark stain of blood, a dark shadowy suggestion of the pain they would now all need to bear together.

Still, she smiled quietly to herself, it was easier to bear now that she had Arthur. He was so kind and gentle with her, and such a gentleman. She paused for a moment, wiped her sore wet hands on her apron, and touched the ring on the little chain around her neck. Surely May was ready now to take on more responsibilities and look after the boys, surely now she could begin to relinquish this burden and set a date.

She smiled again. Next summer. Her hands closed around the ring like a lucky charm.

May sat on the bed and carefully unrolled the silk stockings Lydia had lent her up her slim legs, trying hard not to snag them with the hard little diamonds on her ring. When she had finished, she jumped up and twirled in front of the mirror she and her sister shared, grinning happily as her embroidered skirt flew out as she spun.

Everybody had been so pleased for her when she and Jimmy had walked into the pub last night and told them they were engaged to be married. Her only regret was that Stanley was not there to hear her grand announcement, but later when they walked round the back of the shop, closed at last for the night, he had rewarded her by swinging her off her feet into a bear hug.

She couldn't see the shadow of worry on his face over her

shoulder, and when he put her down, he swallowed hard, smiled brightly, and shook Jimmy's hand.

Jimmy had promised her a night out. Up with the bright lights, where you belong, he'd said.

When he arrived, he smiled at his beautifully dressed little fiancée and kissed her shyly in front of her family, Lydia clicked reprovingly, but then hugged them both, unable to keep up her stern front and grinning over Jimmy's shoulder at her radiant little sister who seemed to be glowing with excitement and pride.

'Have a lovely night, don't be too late,' she called as they walked jauntily out of the door.

They went up town, May marvelling at the crowds of people and the bright lights of the West End. It was payday and Jimmy was feeling flush, he wanted to show his pretty fiancée off to the world. He took May's hand as they stepped off the bus, and May felt herself flush with sudden joy as she looked up at his proud face, smiling down at her.

The dance hall off Oxford Street was packed with people, all looking for fun and ready to forget the daily grind of a working week. Jimmy was a good dancer and May a quick learner, responding eagerly and naturally to his lead, and they soon worked up a thirst as he spun her around the floor.

Smiling with pleasure, May leant back into his embrace, enjoying his casual confidence, relishing the admiring glances from the crowded floor. He swung her again, and with the lightest of touches pulled her hips against his, locking his eyes with hers. She shivered with an unknown sensation, up till now unrecognised and unlooked for, the desire coursing through her like fire. She gasped as he suddenly spun her again, then collapsed laughing into his arms as the music ended, enjoying the feeling as people around them enthusiastically clapped their performance. Jimmy laughed too and for a moment the spell was broken, but May could still feel the warmth within, giddy with this new experience.

'Fancy a drink?' He leaned close to her ear and she nodded, breathlessly, but as she went to find them a seat, she jumped with surprise as another hand closed on her wrist, a voice saying cheerfully, 'C'mon love, have a dance with me, you can't dance just with one person all night!'

May turned to see a man grinning cheekily at her, and before she knew it, he was whirling her out on to the floor, and although she did twist and look for Jimmy, smiling vaguely towards the smoky little bar in case he was looking for her, soon she was enjoying herself in the beat of the music. As soon as the dance finished though, she disentangled herself laughingly from her cheerful and distinctly merry partner and went to find him.

She couldn't see him anywhere. He was not by the bar, nor by the tables where they had sat earlier, but as she scanned the room, she noticed a door open onto the street. He must have stepped out for a bit of fresh air, she thought, trying to ignore a tiny niggle of anxiety in the back of her mind.

She stepped nervously out into the cool night air and took a few deep breaths, enjoying the coolness after the smoky heat of the dance floor. She looked one way but could not see him, then began to turn back to look down the other end of the dark alley, a little reluctant to walk down into the shadows where anyone might be lurking.

And in that next, heart-stopping moment, she saw him. Saw him, not her kind, sweet Jimmy, but a vision of fury as he stepped out of the shadows she had been afraid of and lunged at her, his face contorted into an ugly mask of rage.

'You dirty little bitch!' he hissed. 'How dare you show me up like that, how dare you, May, you little tart!'

Horrified, she saw him raise his hand, and lurched back in a desperate scramble to escape the vicious blow that he aimed at her, knocking her head painfully against the wall as she flinched away. And as he loomed over and came at her again, in her abject terror she felt a shameful hot rush of urine down her legs, down her beautiful stockings and spattering onto the ground.

The blow never fell. Jimmy blinked and stepped back, the anger suddenly leaving him, visibly deflating as he saw her distress and terror, saw her cowering with fear as she leant against the wall for support.

'Oh God May, what have I done? I'm so sorry!' He began to stutter, whimpering the words as he tried to gather her protesting against him, forcing her against his chest as she tried desperately to stand, the roar of blood in her ears making her sway.

'Sweetheart I didn't mean to hurt you, did you fall? I didn't mean to push you, I tried to stop you falling, I tried to stop you!'

He was gabbling now, almost incoherent with his apologies, and shakily May pulled away from him, nauseated by a wave of pain and confusion. She stared up at him blankly, not understanding the words he was saying, nothing seemed to make sense.

Was that what had happened?

'May, please answer me, are you all right? I'm so sorry, I didn't mean to make you jump, I'm sorry you knocked your head,' he said again, his panicky eyes pleading for an answer, for her to believe him.

May made a huge effort to pull herself together, gazing up in bewilderment at the face of the stranger she had promised to marry.

'I'm all right,' she answered weakly, 'you gave me an awful fright though. Please Jimmy, can we just go home now?'

He walked her home, solicitous, loving. Lying.

And May walked next to him, arm in arm but a thousand miles away, not daring to tell him her damp shoes were chafing with every step, reeling with confusion and humiliation.

As she tiptoed into the girls' room, Lydia stirred and rolled towards her, blinking blearily.

'Did you have a lovely time?' she mumbled sleepily.

'Lovely,' agreed May, automatically.

She peeled off her ruined stockings and dropped them wordlessly into the bin.

The next day, May awoke with a dull headache pressing behind her eyes, and rolled over with a groan. Snapshots of the evening had run through her mind relentlessly through the night like a silent movie show, flickering in an eerie, silent and seemingly endless nightmare.

She groaned again, unsure if she could possibly be remembering it right. Surely he hadn't tried to hit her? Maybe she had just tripped after all; now she winced guiltily when she thought of her strappy high heels, surely he must have lunged to catch her. She must, must surely have mistaken his intentions.

That was it. That must have been what happened, after all, that's what her Jimmy had said, wasn't it, and after all, he had looked after her so well on the way home. She sighed with relief, she had finally managed to get it straight in her mind, and now it all made perfect sense.

'May!' Her sister's exasperated voice sounded from the kitchen downstairs, and she sat up with a start, and called back to Lydia, 'I'll be down in a minute.'

When she went downstairs, her elder sister was waiting for her with a grim look on her face.

'So, May,' asked Lydia, acidly, 'where exactly are my stockings?'

May stared at her, appalled. What could she possibly say? The suppressed memory of last night's humiliation arose in her mind, and suddenly her cheeks burned with shame. A grown woman, yet at nineteen years old she had wet herself just like a child, in front of her fiancé and now even her sister seemed to know. She looked down, unable to meet Lydia's accusing eyes.

Lydia snorted. 'I thought as much. What would Mum have said to you now, carrying on like that and you two not even with a date set yet?'

May looked up and stared at her, uncomprehending. What Lydia had not yet grasped was that, losing her mother so young, May had never had the facts of life explained nor even hinted at. Lydia herself had been told all the gory details, as yet unsampled for herself, by their older cousin, Hetty, but had never seen fit to enlighten May. And poles apart, mortified by a different event she was too embarrassed to confess, May hadn't the slightest idea what Lydia was talking about at all.

'Well you'd best get a wriggle on now,' said Lydia, the ghost of a grin appearing on her cross face, 'better let him walk you down the aisle as quick as you can!'

Cast adrift and far out of her depth, May felt an icy-cold hand clamp around her heart.

No escape.

There was no turning back now.

Stanley burst abruptly into the kitchen with a clatter of boots on the scrubbed floorboards. A stew was bubbling on the stove and a ray of sunlight was shining through the window where Lydia was standing at the sink as usual, and she turned round startled, not used to seeing anyone in the house during the day.

'Whatever is it, Stanley?' She asked worriedly, noting his flushed face and dishevelled appearance, it was so unlike him to leave the shop unattended.

Stanley tried to catch his breath, 'I've just heard it on the wireless, Lyd. There's going to be a war!'

Lydia stared at him. War rumours had been flying round for months, and she was used to her brothers hotly discussing them as they returned from the pub every Friday night. Hitler, the Brown Shirts, the Sudetenland, all of these new names and words were on everybody's tongue.

But on the wireless? That made it real.

'But we're not at war now, are we?' she asked, her voice ragged with sudden anxiety.

'Not yet, no,' admitted Stanley, 'but it really sounds like things are hotting up! That Mr Hitler can't just keep doing what he's doing without getting his comeuppance, somebody's got to stop him!'

'It's not a game, Stanley,' retorted Lydia angrily. 'You boys go on about it like you're playing tin soldiers but I, for one, don't want there to be another war!'

She spun away from him, wiping her face abruptly with her apron, as unwanted memories of Dad suddenly welled up in her mind.

Dad, such a proud and strong man, broken by his time serving on the Western Front. Disintegrating utterly after their mother died, searching for solace in the depths of a bottle, the rest of their extended family calling him a disgrace for turning to drink rather than seeing him as a single father and the struggling, lonely, desperate soldier that he had been. She shuddered when she thought of him slamming back home from the pub to open another bottle, then another, sitting at the kitchen table like an dark raincloud ready to vent his fury on anyone who passed too near. Remembering how she had to shoo the little ones out of his sight, terrified he would hit out, taking them upstairs to mop up milk with bread in a bowl because she had been too afraid to venture back down to prepare a proper meal. At his funeral, his orphaned children had stood at his graveside, alone and unsupported by friends and family alienated by his behaviour in the months before he died. As they said goodbye to their father, they had held hands for a moment, their little family standing lonely but proud against the world. Closing ranks.

'It's not a game,' she repeated, looking up into the eyes of the little brother she had brought up as her own baby, and seeing her fear, Stanley reached to give her a hard hug, ashamed that he hadn't thought what this would mean for her, a child and victim in her own way of the last war.

'Sorry, sis,' he muttered awkwardly, 'I just needed to tell someone, that's all. It's really quiet in the shop today.'

She looked at him tenderly. She knew that Stanley was chafing against the shop these days, wishing he had something more to occupy his mind. She knew that he loved nothing better than to draw, she had seen him sketching away late at night while the others were at the pub, and his stuff was good, really good. Her heart went out to him, he had a talent going to waste because the family needed his strength to stack shelves and there was no room in their lives for an artistic temperament. So poor Stanley gritted his teeth and got on with it, but she and May knew where his dreams took him when he sat down with his finely sharpened pencil and let it fly over the paper.

'You need to get back to the shop, lovey,' she chided him, reluctantly.

He straightened his shoulders and looked at her, bleakly.

'I know, I'll go now. But I'm finishing up on time tonight, I have something I need to do.'

With that, he turned on his heel and left, leaving his sister wondering what on earth he could have meant.

Bert and Reggie were already in the pub as Stanley locked up the shop. They both knew they should help him more, but both of them were busy with their own jobs as well as doing the shop's accounts, and felt that their after-work pint was well justified and a sacred ritual indeed.

Reggie looked up from his beer in surprise as his younger brother walked in just a few minutes later.

'You're early today, Stanley!' he exclaimed. 'Everything all right?'

Stanley looked at him, squarely. 'Yes, everything's fine. I'll be over in a tick.'

Reggie and Bert watched him with fond smiles as he turned and walked purposefully up to the bar and waited for service, but Millie had already spotted him and came over at once, smiling shyly at him over the bar.

'What'll it be?' she asked, encouragingly.

Stanley raised his eyes to meet hers and looked at her for a long moment, his mouth dry and his courage almost deserting him. Then, with a huge effort, cleared his throat and said firmly,

'I'd like to ask you out for a drink sometime.'

There. It was done. In the tiny silence that followed his request, he could have sworn he heard a pin drop, and wished wildly that he could take back the words he had uttered and make them more memorable, more romantic somehow, before hazily realising that she had already answered him, the 'yes' bending her sweet lips into a beautiful smile. In fact, she was looking at him, amazed at his steadiness and his determination when her heart was fluttering so hard she was sure he would be able to hear it.

'Yes. I'd like that very much,' Millie repeated quietly, smiling up at him.

When Stanley joined his brothers a moment later, a pint in his hand and joy in his heart, Reggie and Bert discreetly failed to comment when his trembling hand spilled beer on the table, acutely aware that their baby brother had just grown up.

Millie drifted through the rest of her shift, humming happily to herself in a blissful daze. She couldn't quite believe it, she hadn't trusted her ears when Stanley had asked her out. She blushed when she remembered how she'd nearly asked him to say it again, but then smiled joyfully when she thought of the resolve in his voice when he'd straightened his shoulders and looked her directly in the eye.

Stanley might be the youngest brother, she thought to herself, but he was a man in his own right, standing firmly on his own two feet.

She did wonder, briefly, what had made him change from his usual mumbled drinks order to this forthright request, then put it out of her mind.

After all, with the leaders of the world still in denial, it was hardly surprising that, like so many of her age, she had no inkling of the storm that was about to break across Europe and across her world.

The winter gave way to spring, and gradually a new pattern of life emerged for the young couples.

May and Jimmy became more and more popular and increasingly proficient on the dance floor, other dancers preferring to become mere spectators whenever they took to the floor.

The memory of that terrible night was fading rapidly. May was convinced now that she had misinterpreted the situation, that she must indeed have slipped in her high heels and that Jimmy had lunged to save her. He adored her. Every time he looked at her, the intensity of his feelings shone through, almost singeing her with their power. She was mesmerised by him, moving in a dream towards their wedding day, which, after deep and urgent discussion with Hetty, Lydia had arranged for the end of April, just a few short months away.

Stanley and Millie became an item, and seemed to fit snugly into each other's lives as if they had always been together. She could always be found at the front of the shop each day as he was cashing up, humming cheerfully under her breath as she scrubbed down the step and polished the brass door handle. Then much later, Stanley would start collecting glasses up at the end of the evening after last orders had been called at the pub, having a joke and a laugh with the late drinkers but keeping a sharp eye out for any trouble. After she had closed up he would walk her home holding hands, both marvelling at the peaceable joy they had come to find in each other's company.

He had begun to sketch her, tentative at first, shy even to ask. But then he found his talent would overtake his awkwardness, his deft hand sketching rapidly and decisively, catching fleeting poses, sudden changes of mood.

Millie was enthralled by him, captivated by his passion and skill. They grew ever closer, marvelling that such a short time ago they had never even spoken, revelling in this new intimacy.

Lydia and Arthur met when they could, which wasn't often enough for either of them. Lydia fretted at her role of mother figure, which now seemed nothing more than housekeeper to a household who no longer appreciated her, beyond the simple but unnoticed and unacknowledged pleasure of returning to good wholesome food in a shabby but spotlessly clean home. Arthur's shift work at the local railway station made it hard to see him, but then again, she thought slyly, it did mean sometimes he would drop in unexpectedly for some precious, unchaperoned hours. He was always very proper, but only up to a point, she thought to herself, blushing as she remembered the feel of his lips on hers and his hands crushing her against his lean body. She sniffed, unbidden tears rising in the back of her throat.

So unfair that silly May got to have all the fun, and as a result got to have the early wedding she had dreamed of for herself. But the family could hardly stretch to hosting two weddings this year, could it, she thought bitterly, so once again, her desires went unvoiced and her dreams put on hold.

This was to be May's moment, and all she could do was stand aside magnanimously and watch her baby sister outshine them all.

The 17th of April dawned chilly and bright, the air crisp in May's lungs as she took a deep, steadying breath at the window.

Today was her special day, hers and Jimmy's. Her beautiful dress hung from the wardrobe door, the tiny, sparkly rosebuds she had embroidered catching the early morning light. She had stitched every bit of the dress from scratch. Jimmy had already told her they must start saving their money so that they could move out of the big family house on Muswell Hill and get their own little place, so dutifully she had unravelled other clothes and picked off the lace from Lydia's generously donated blouse to sew around the neckline. The rosebuds were her only extravagance, each one lovingly embroidered with silver and pink thread she had saved hard to buy from her savings. Her job at the dressmakers didn't pay well, but at least they let her have this at cost, so she hadn't seen the point in mentioning it to Jimmy.

She shuddered and swayed suddenly, almost swamped by a complex wave of emotion: excitement and dread combined in a heady mixture that threatened darkly to overwhelm her. But staring at her pale face in the mirror and, taking a few, calming breaths, she turned deliberately and slipped the wedding dress over her head.

The soft pink chiffon clung to her body, making her look elegant and sophisticated, yet unbearably childlike in the same instant. Like her brothers and sister, her hair was black, and her hazel eyes slanted up mysteriously or mischievously as the mood took her. She stared at herself curiously in the mirror, lost in thought as she contemplated the beautiful stranger before her.

A long, low wolf whistle interrupted her reverie, and she looked up with a start into the eyes of her eldest brother.

'Ready?' Reggie said with a determined grin, blinking back the tears as he looked down at his youngest sister and realising with a sudden lurch how like Edie she looked, sensing the loss of his closest sibling for the first time in years. Not even Bert really remembered her now, and Reggie felt sad as he realised that some of their family history was beginning to disappear with time as they all grew up and moved on.

'Ready,' she replied quietly, wondering if that could ever be true.

In reality she felt a little dizzy, and again had the bizarre sensation of walking through fog. A sense of inevitability, not of the excitement of a young girl who had chosen her dream, out to embrace it through her own free will.

But she knew how much this day had cost Lydia, both in real terms and in emotional, and she knew that she couldn't let her down. She had convinced herself that her path was ordained the night she had got so confused and had upset Jimmy, and she could only thank Lydia for saving her reputation and letting her have this early wedding, utterly unaware still of Lydia's motives for this.

She smiled gamely up at Reggie, determined not to let the side down with the tears she knew were threatening. She swallowed hard. 'Let's go then,' she said brightly, and walked out into the brittle, hard light of the morning.

Years later, in the periods of latter quiet they shared when age began to temper their pride, Lydia would ask her, 'What were you thinking as you walked down that aisle?'

'I've gone and done it now,' she had replied abruptly, turning away from the sudden pity in her sister's eyes, never recognising the guilt she harboured there.

The service passed in a moment, May aware of Jimmy's eyes locked with hers, full of adoration. Suddenly they were all back in the rarely used front room of the big house, eating the tiny crusty sandwiches and pies she, Lydia and Hetty had worked so hard to prepare the night before. As she had expected, Jimmy swung her into his arms and began to dance as Bert struck up a tune on his accordion, and soon they were all clapping in time to the music as he spun her expertly around the floor.

May finally began to relax and enjoy herself as she and Jimmy danced ever closer and more in tune with one another than ever. A catlike smile began to spread across her face, after all, this was what they were good at together. In answer, Jimmy smiled down at her and kissed her on the lips, sending an unexpected jolt of sensation down her spine, and pulled her closer as he felt the tremor spread through her body.

'Time for bed?' He leant and whispered in her ear suggestively, emboldened by the sweet white wine Bert and Reggie had appropriated through Millie's landlord.

She smiled up at him trustingly, unsuspecting and innocent. She knew no more than she had before she met him, neither elder sister nor cousin had yet recognised the need to elaborate, both convinced she was already well versed in this particular department.

'Let's go up,' she agreed.

And so Jimmy and May swept triumphantly up the stairs to the cheering bawdiness and then bashful laughter of the family. Headed hand in hand to their new bedroom which had once belonged to her parents and then to Lydia, who had now tactfully retreated to May's old room which had little privacy being just above the kitchen.

Alone at last, she twirled for him, sparkling as she went through the door, and laughing, he caught her up in his arms and carried her over the little wooden threshold. The two of them held each other tight for one beautiful, perfect moment that May would remember for ever. Then her young husband strode over to the bed and laid her down reverently, smiling at her and drinking in her beauty with loving eyes.

It was then that he noticed the silver thread on the rosebuds.

The newlyweds did not emerge from their bedroom at all the next morning, and Lydia smiled ruefully at her own jealousy as she put a plate of sandwiches and tea on the landing and rapped on the door before retreating briskly back down the stairs.

But when Stanley saw May creeping back inside from the privy that evening when he got back from the shop, he saw the strain on her face and knew instinctively, as he always had known with his twin, that she was far from being a happy bride.

'May—' He reached his arms out to her, and thankfully she fell into his familiar embrace and rested her head against his shoulder, just as she always had. May closed her eyes, relief flooding through her and opened her mouth to confide in him, desperate to share what had happened. Then to his utter dismay, Stanley felt her stiffen suddenly and, with a subtle shift, withdrew from his raw concern with her lips tightly clamped.

'What is it, love?' he asked tenderly, still hoping to recapture the moment.

She shuddered at the gentleness in his voice, then gathered herself and looked him straight in the eye.

'I'm tired, that's all!' she riposted gaily, to the twin brother she had shared a womb and a childhood with. 'I'm a married woman now, you know!'

Confused, Stanley went to pull her around to face him directly, horrified to see her wince as his hand closed on her wrist.

Her bruised wrist.

The anger rose inside him like bile. May, his little, baby sister, bruised from her wedding night. The sheer wrongness of this made him breathless with rage, but he calmed himself enough to ask gently, knowing he had to help her tell him the truth: 'What happened, lovey?' Then, to his utter consternation, she smiled. Smiled with all the joy of a grimacing skeleton, her familiar and much loved features stretching into a shocking and bizarre parody of happiness.

'Nothing happened, I'm fine! I just bumped against the table when we were dancing last night.'

And with a tiny, heartbreakingly proud little flounce, the person he had known and loved best twisted away from him and retreated back up to her newly closed door.

Stanley had little time over the next few days to discuss his fears with anyone, even if he had felt that he had anything tangible to talk about.

A new coal delivery came into the shop and had to be distributed to those who had placed their orders. Reggie and Bert were rarely around now anyway, both disappearing back to their own lives after the flurry of their baby sister's special day. Millie was rushed off her feet with the annual spring clean at the pub, and Lydia was doing the same in the big house.

Neither Jimmy nor May were given any leave after their wedding, so both were back to their normal routine after the weekend, May dashing off to catch her bus to the dressmakers, Jimmy jauntily walking the half-mile to the busy little workshop as if he hadn't a care in the world.

With spring blossoming, Stanley began to wonder if his fears for May were unfounded. She seemed happy enough, always in a rush but bright and bubbly as ever. Jimmy was working extra shifts down at the workshop, and was now pretty much running the repairs side of the garage. He and May didn't go out much now, May had confided that they were saving to move into their own place as soon as possible.

Stanley sighed when he thought of little May moving out,

moving on. All the same, he reflected grimly, with all this talk of war, maybe they would all need to move on soon, one way or another.

He smiled to himself then, thinking fondly of Millie and how far they had come since that first date. He was so glad that he had shown her his drawings, and that she had then offered to model for him. He had drawn her so many times now, he felt he knew every inch of her; that is, the inches she allowed him to see, he grinned wryly to himself. He felt that they complemented each other perfectly, Millie impetuous and full of fun, the foil to his darkness, his quiet reserve.

Smiling to himself, he let himself out of the back door of the shop and locked up. It was Wednesday, early closing day, and he was meeting Millie. He couldn't wait to see her, the drawing he had planned had been on the edge of his consciousness all day, slowly taking shape in his mind.

If only she would let him.

Millie smiled and ran to him when he knocked at the door. She had been on tenterhooks all morning waiting for him to call around, and had spent hours choosing what to wear to please him most. In the end, she had plumped for a simple but pretty outfit, her favourite white blouse and full blue skirt tightly cinched in with a narrow black belt, but couldn't help but wince a little as she struggled to walk in the high heels a friend had kindly lent her for the occasion. When Stanley's eye fell upon her, she noted the admiration on his face and smiled, a little flustered, as he returned her grin and bent to plant a chaste kiss on her cheek.

Recovering herself swiftly, she asked cheekily, 'So what's for lunch?' knowing that he had a surprise in store. In answer, he smiled triumphantly and held out what he'd been hiding behind his back with a flourish, and Millie squealed with delight when she saw the little picnic hamper and tartan rug tied to the top.

'But I thought you said you wanted to draw some more?' she asked, puzzled.

'I do, I do,' laughed Stanley, 'but it's sunny and I fancied some fresh air.'

Millie smiled up at him in agreement and they walked out together into the sun, holding hands a little shyly in the bright sunlight. Without needing to say, they both turned up the hill towards the palace and its beautiful grounds, so perfect for a picnic on this peaceful, balmy day.

As Stanley unpacked the food, he smiled at Millie lying back in the sun, greedily soaking up the early summer's rays all curled up like a self-satisfied kitten on the little rug. He put his arm round her cautiously while they were eating and was relieved to felt her relax against him, marvelling again at how far they had come in the last few months, how afraid he had been even to talk to her to order a pint at the bar.

When they had finished their sandwiches, Millie leant back against the tree and sighed.

'It's so beautiful here,' she whispered, looking over at him seriously, 'and so lovely just being quiet with you and no one else for a change!'

In answer, Stanley rolled over and kissed her, this time on the lips. Millie had closed her eyes momentarily and gasped with surprise at his touch, then returned his kiss inexpertly but with fervour. After a moment though, his head reeling, Stanley shuddered and pulled away, shocked at the power of his feelings, and needing to break the contact to collect himself. Breathing fast, Millie waited, unwilling to break the spell and aware of the solemnity of the moment. There wasn't a soul in sight, they seemed to have the palace gardens to themselves.

'Millie,' he said urgently, imperative now in his need, his desire for her, 'can I draw you?'

She nodded, like him well aware that they were alone, and silenced by the strength of her feelings.

She sat up shakily, then leant back against the tree again to watch as he got out his sketch pad and pencil. He looked at her intently for a long moment, then began to sketch, silently and swiftly as always.

Millie watched him, aware of his keen gazes, then knew without needing to question it, what she would do next. Slowly, deliberately, she undid the top buttons of her blouse, then shrugged her shoulders so it fell down, exposing the bare skin of her throat.

Stanley froze, spellbound as he watched her fiddling with the tiny buttons. Then, wordlessly, he reached over and gently pulled the cotton lower so he could see the curve of her breasts, her tiny waist and soft stomach, pale in the bright light of the sun She smiled up at him, tremulously, then took a deep breath and shut her eyes.

'Millie?' Stanley asked hoarsely, struggling to contain himself as he drank in the sight of her young body, offered so shyly and so sweetly as she'd done. She opened her eyes again and reached up to kiss him fervently.

'Now draw me!' she giggled suddenly, and the tension dispersed as he picked up his pencil and let it caress the curves of her body as he committed the memory of her to paper forever.

Hours later, Stanley stopped and Millie stretched luxuriously on the rug, marvelling at herself that she could be so relaxed now in her near nakedness, sublimely happy in his company. He smiled at her.

'Do you want to see?' he asked, teasingly. She returned his grin and sat up, pulling her blouse back into place and winked mischievously at him as she buttoned it back up. Then she glanced over at his sketch book, and gasped, captivated. Every feature, every nuance of her body captured by the loving, skilled strokes of his pencil, her nakedness exposed but in the most innocent of ways, her youth and beauty shining from the page.

'It's so beautiful,' she exclaimed, and in that moment, Stanley leant over and kissed her again. Then he drew back sharply and looked at her sheepishly.

'We'd better go back,' he said quietly, 'but thank you for letting me draw you, I've been wanting to for such a long time, love.'

They packed up their belongings and walked in silence back through the gardens towards Muswell Hill. Just before they reached Millie's house, they stopped and kissed again, Millie's arms wrapped tightly around his neck, and in the coming months, Stanley would always remember that moment as the last perfect moment before everything he held dear was changed for ever and the world about them went mad.

Part Three

1939, Changes

When he stepped through the back door into the kitchen, Stanley felt the atmosphere immediately, just as surely as if the temperature had suddenly plummeted.

May was sitting at the table, still and ashen-faced, two bolts of cloth lying next to her. Jimmy was standing over her, his face also white but angry, and Stanley could see his fists clenching and sensed that he must have just been shouting. Lydia was standing frozen by the sink, anxiously wringing a tea-towel over and over with her wet hands, relief washing over her taut features when she saw Stanley walk in.

He dragged his eyes away from May's stricken face and looked at Lydia, questioningly.

'May's lost her job,' she said, and with that both she and May burst into tears, Lydia noisily, May almost silently, her shoulders shaking with distress. When Jimmy made no move to comfort her,

Stanley moved to her side, pulled her to her feet and put his arms round her, horrified to feel her whole body trembling with the effort to control herself.

Over the next few minutes, it all came out. In shuddering breaths, May told him what had happened, Jimmy stalking across the kitchen to stand rigidly with his arms crossed at the bottom of the stairs, listening stony-faced as his wife wept.

May's boss was Jewish, and like so many Jews in London, he had begun to fear the stories they were hearing more and more from the wireless. His dressmaker's business had begun to suffer since the spring, his wealthy clients tending to shy away from po-tential scandal, any possible hint of trouble, and choosing to stay away from the well-known and previously popular Jew.

'He's shut down the shop,' whispered May, piteously, 'he told me he was sorry but there was no more work for me and he's going to leave London straight away. He gave me some material instead of last week's pay, he said he hasn't got anything left to pay me with.' Her sob caught in her throat and she looked at Stanley desperately, 'and me and Jimmy are SAVING and now I haven't got a job!'

She broke down again, and Stanley scowled furiously across at Jimmy, who deliberately avoided his eyes.

'Right, that's enough now,' he said briskly, taking control. Af-ter all, if Jimmy wouldn't, why shouldn't he, he wondered angrily. May looked up at him, surprised by his sudden purposeful tone. 'Go wash your face, May, you need to get job-hunting right away!'

May sniffed and then straightened up, wiping her tears with the fingers.

'You're right,' she said, rallying, 'I need to get a wriggle on and get out there. It was just such a shock though, and I feel so sorry for Mr Segal too, he's such a nice man and he was so upset.'

Stanley nodded grimly, Mr Segal was not the first Jew to be having troubles in London, and he felt that he wouldn't be the last, the way people were talking down the pub. He pushed May gently towards Jimmy, who grudgingly – or was that just Stanley's anger playing tricks on him? – took her hand to lead her upstairs.

Lydia smiled at him gratefully when they were gone.

'I'm so glad you came home then,' she said. 'Jimmy was being so hateful, he was shouting at her and it really wasn't her fault, you'd have thought she did it to spite him.'

And in that next instant, sister and brother stood transfixed with horror as they both heard a crash from upstairs, a muffled scream, then a yawning, dreadful silence.

Stanley was the first to recover his wits, and ran upstairs two at a time, hammering on May and Jimmy's closed door and shouting for them to open up. Abruptly, the door swung open, and Jimmy stood looking at him coldly.

'What's your problem, mate?' he asked rudely, but Stanley was in no mood to talk, and pushed straight past him and into the room, then stopped suddenly, taken aback by the normality of the scene before his eyes.

May was sitting on the chair in the bay window, buckling her best high heels onto her tiny feet. She looked calm and although she did have two high spots of colour on her cheeks, she appeared unruffled, and Stanley felt his fear deflating, stood there feeling silly and confused.

'I thought I heard a bang,' he muttered, trying desperately to look into her eyes to connect with her at some deeper level, to understand what was happening in her life, which she seemed at pains to keep so private since her marriage. To his chagrin, she dropped her eyes from his gaze and laughed brightly, and again he wondered if it was only he who could hear the brittle edge to her laughter.

'I'm fine, Stanley, I just dropped the flat iron in the grate.' He looked over and sure enough, the flat iron seemed to have fallen from its stand, ash scattered around it in the grate.

'So long as you're all right then,' he said gruffly, and stepping past Jimmy, he retreated reluctantly back down the stairs where Lydia was waiting anxiously to hear what was going on.

He looked at her helplessly, stumped by the lack of evidence, but sure at a level so visceral that it hurt him to breathe, that something was very wrong with his twin, his little sister. He explained haltingly to Lydia what he had seen, and for the first time, tried to describe the utter wrongness of what he could feel, struggling to find the right words but convinced he was right to be afraid for her. Lydia listened intently to each, hesitant word, and she bit her lip anxiously.

'We just have to watch and wait,' she said quietly. 'If there's something wrong, surely she'll tell us? Jimmy seems so sweet…' Her voice trailed off uncertainly, and she looked at Stanley with guilty tears starting in her eyes.

'I encouraged her to marry him,' she confessed, horrified by her thoughts now, remembering how she'd urged May, ordered May, to set an early date.

Stanley gave her a firm hug then, needing her to stop her journey into self-castigation.

'May made that decision all by herself,' he countered grimly. 'We just have to help her live with it.'

The next day, May woke with a sudden jolt, realising she must have awakened when Jimmy shut the door, leaving for work earlier and earlier so that he could book in more and more jobs. She sighed sadly, what was wrong with living in the big house anyway, didn't they have enough space as it was? Her eyes filled with tears suddenly as she tried to envisage leaving the house where she'd been born, leaving and setting up home without Stanley and Lydia. She was not at all sure she was ready for that.

She lay still for a few more moments, reluctant to face the day, then opened her eyes, disorientated. She never slept on her front as a rule, but strangely she had awakened this way and felt stiff as a board. Gingerly she went to shrug off the blanket, then winced as the sheet seemed to catch on her back. She pushed herself up with an effort, then froze, horrified as she saw blood on the sheet, dark blood congealing and sticking the rough cotton against her bare flesh. The pain from her back was raw, unexpected, and sickness almost overcame her. She had fallen asleep in Jimmy's contrite arms and she'd blocked out what he'd done to her yesterday with the strap of his belt, her mind closing down on itself again now, struggling with the enormity of trying to find a way to forget, a way to forgive.

Easier not to think at all.

Suddenly she remembered her task for the days ahead, she needed to find a job as fast as possible. Gritting her teeth against the pain, she peeled the sheet away from her lacerated skin as gently as she could, and trying to pull herself together, sat up quickly, gasping as the room reeled around her. Gingerly, she got out of bed, then went to the washstand to splash her face. She glared at the pale reflection in the old, cracked mirror hanging over the stand on a nail, and scolded herself.

'Come on, May, there's no point in crying over spilt milk,' she chided herself, then picked up her make-up and began to apply it like war paint, ready to do battle with the world.

Lydia turned as May walked into the kitchen, ready to console, ready to hear what had happened, ready to try to stem the hurt just like she had when May was a little girl and she her surrogate mother, patching up her scratches with iodine and dressings. But her mouth dropped open when she saw her, her appearance so utterly at odds with her expectations that she was rendered speechless for a long, disorientated moment.

'Where are you going, all dressed up to the nines?' she managed lamely.

May looked radiant. Her dress was tightly cinched in round her waist, and the skirt flowed out revealing her shapely legs and high heels. She tilted her chin up defiantly, stared at Lydia, and declared,

'Job-hunting, of course. Me and Jimmy want our own place so I need to get earning again so we can save up.'

And with that she stalked towards the door and out on to the street, Lydia's called suggestion about breakfast falling on deaf ears as she went out to rejoin the workforce as soon as ever she could.

As soon as she was out of the door, May drew a long, ragged breath and blinked hard to clear the tears and the faintness threatening to blur her vision. It had been so, so hard to rebuff the succour Lydia was offering her, not to run into her arms for the comfort she craved. But she had married Jimmy, for better or for worse, she reflected grimly, and she had to accept her lot in life. She glanced down at herself critically and straightened her belt, wincing as the material of her dress rubbed against the weals on her back, then strode off with her heels clicking determinedly in the direction of Bond Street, where everyone knew that all the finest seamstresses worked.

Hours later, footsore and dejected, she stood outside yet another dressmaker's. This one was larger than the others, and even more intimidating that they had been, made worse by the terrible racket that emanated from the windows opening onto the street. May tried to pluck up her courage, knowing with a deep sinking feeling in her stomach how much worse it would be to go home tonight to Jimmy, jobless and dependent.

She climbed the steps to the big double door, walked in and stopped abruptly. The dressmaker's was more of a factory to her eyes, rows and rows of bolts of cloth down one side, then more rows of tables with machines, electric machines, she noted with horror, with scores of girls of all ages working with their heads down, chattering nineteen to the dozen.

'Can I help you?' boomed a voice behind her, and May nearly jumped out of her skin, so absorbed had she been in the scene below her.

May took a deep, steadying breath, then told the kindly look-ing man that she was looking for work, that she was a good seam-stress, and that she had lost her job due to the her boss leaving town.

'Jewish, was he?' wondered the man out loud, then looking at her astutely, 'Can you work on electric?'

May gulped, then nodded firmly.

'Oh yes, I've been using electric for years,' she said airily, crossing her fingers behind her back, quite determined to get this job at all costs.

'Excellent,' beamed the man, 'we can always use girls trained on electric machines. Janie, come over here and get this new girl sorted out with a machine, get her stitching some hems so we can see what she's made of.'

A slim young girl, about May's age, detached herself from her own machine and came over to them. She smiled at May and beckoned for her to come over to the machinists' tables, sat her down before an unused machine and went back to her own work at the table opposite. May eyed the contraption with alarm, trying vainly to conceal her trepidation. Eventually, she looked up and caught Janie's eye, who returned the look with sympathy.

'Um,' ventured May reluctantly, 'I've never threaded up this particular model before, could you show me?'

Janie obligingly swung out of her seat again and came across to her, and with a few deft moves, threaded up the machine, May watching avidly, trying to memorise every detail.

'There you go,' she said cheerfully, 'just give me a holler if you need any help.'

She went back to her seat and within seconds was sewing again, running a long straight seam along the material she was working with. May watched surreptitiously for a few more moments, then took a deep breath and turned to her machine. It looked very much like the Singer she was used to in some respects, but instead of a wrought iron treadle at her feet, she had a small white pedal on a wire. Carefully, she placed the material Janie had given her under the needle, then pressed down experimentally with her foot. To her abject horror, the material whirred out of her fingers at enormous speed, and she let out an involuntary shriek as it all bunched up under her shaking fingers.

Blessedly, Janie was at her side again, and all of a sudden the two of them were in fits of laughter, clutching at their sides and gasping for breath as they surveyed May's handiwork.

'You've never used one of these before, have you?!' Janie challenged her, wiping away the tears of mirth with the back of her hands. May shook her head, unable to speak past the gales of hysterical giggles that were still welling up inside of her.

'Don't worry, Mr Courtney guessed anyway, that's why he asked me to help,' explained Janie. 'Hardly anywhere else in London has electric machines you see, so whatever you told him, he saw straight through you.'

'So why did he offer me the job then?' wondered May, and Janie leaned over to her, conspiratorially.

'There's going to be a war, don't you see? So they'll be needing uniforms and lots of them. Who best to provide for the government besides a busy factory that already has girls trained on electric?'

May stared at her, hearing the sense in her words, but afraid she might be right.

'You'd better show me again then!' she said determinedly, and turned back to her machine.

Jimmy shifted uncomfortably under the truck he was working on. The day was hot and the sweat was running in his eyes as he tried to squint at the faulty brake calliper he was trying to work loose. He was struggling to concentrate, if he was honest, but then again, Jimmy was rarely honest with himself, because he really didn't like what he saw when he tried.

Images of last night kept floating at the edge of his vision, piercing and jabbing at him just like the beginnings of a migraine. May weeping on the bed after he'd struck her with the belt, over and over again, pulling away from him to escape and falling to the floor, upsetting the flat iron in the grate as she did so. Then hearing the sound of Stanley racing up the stairs, watching her incredulously as she immediately composed herself to join him, support him even, in his web of deceit.

Bile rose in his throat and he pulled out from under the truck, swallowing hard and rubbing his eyes with his dirty hands. He had made love to her after Stanley left, desperately proclaiming his love for her, kissing away her protests and declaring her the most wonderful creature he had ever met. Afterwards, she rolled away from him wordlessly, and if she wasn't actually asleep within seconds, then she'd done a pretty good job of feigning it.

'Are you all right, son?' asked a voice behind him, and Jimmy jumped up, glad to be disturbed from his dark thoughts. May shouldn't have made him so angry, he thought to himself self-righteously, it wasn't just up to him to save the money they needed. He nodded at his boss.

'Just taking a breather, Bob,' he said quickly, then rolled back under the truck to the job and his re-worked version of the memories of last night.

When May walked back up Muswell Hill that night towards the big house, her legs were trembling with exhaustion and her fingers were raw with the number of times she had caught them under the vicious needle, flying through the material faster than she knew how to anticipate. Inside, however, her heart was singing. Her first day's wages were clinking in her purse, and more than that, she had made fast friends with Janie, and May recognised instinctively that she needed a friend outside of her family, someone whom she could really talk to without everyone telling her what to do.

She opened the door and as she did so, saw a flurry of movement as Lydia and Arthur detached themselves from a passionate embrace, Lydia's hands flying to cover her scarlet face.

'I'm so sorry,' blurted May awkwardly, then laughed as she saw her elder sister's consternation, 'but we do all know about you though, you know!'

Arthur grinned at her appreciatively, then draped his arm back over Lydia's shoulder, ignoring her discomfiture and giving her a firm squeeze.

'Any luck with the job then?' muttered Lydia, unable to meet her eye, and May smiled jauntily and went over to the jar where they all paid their share of their wages towards the house-keeping.

'I should say so,' she laughed, and tipped in more than her usual share, Mr Courtney being generous especially as she had worked so hard to catch up that long first day. As she did so, she froze as Jimmy walked through the door, his eyes fixed on her purse.

'Clearly a good day then?' he enquired, coolly, then went to go upstairs. May cast a backwards glance at her still blushing sister, then went reluctantly to follow him, realising then just how much she would rather spend time with Lydia and Arthur telling them about her new job and Janie than follow her husband.

As she'd feared, he turned on her as soon as they reached their room.

'How much did you just put in the jar?' he demanded furiously. 'It looked like a lot more than your usual share!'

'It was more than usual because I earned more than usual' she retorted, defiantly, then flinched as he raised his hand to strike her in his rage. 'Please Jimmy, no!'

She cried out, twisting desperately to escape his hard hand, miserably regretting her defiance of the moment before, but fast as a snake, he followed her, grabbing her by her belt, and threw her bodily onto the bed. Frantically, she tried to wriggle off the other side but he was much too fast for her, his face contorted with anger, lashing at her back and her legs with his free hand while he pinned her down with the other.

With every bit of self-control she could muster, May clamped her mouth shut on the screams she was on the verge of making.

She shut her eyes tightly, refusing to acknowledge him, willing her mind to take her away to another place, a quiet, safe place where he could not hurt her. Anywhere but here. Gradually, her body went limp as she stopped resisting him, and all of a sudden, mercifully he stopped, staring down at her still form.

'May?' he whispered, then leaned over to shake her, terrified that he had gone too far, that he had killed her in his fury.

She opened her eyes and looked at him, and he let out a long sigh of relief, then gave way to a storm of weeping. She watched him dispassionately for a while, then made to get up, steeling herself against the pain as she moved. Jimmy wept anew when he saw her painful movements, reached out to hold her against him.

'I'm so sorry, May,' he whimpered softly, 'I didn't mean to hurt you, you shouldn't have made me angry like that.'

She looked at him coldly then, trying to remember why she had thought she'd ever loved him. He began to gabble, sensing her withdrawal, desperate to connect with her anew.

'I just want our own place, I just want it to be just us, I can't live with your family, I just want you!'

'You've never once asked me what I want, have you?' replied May, stonily. His eyes opened wide in astonishment, then he asked, 'So what do you want, May? Do you want to stay here with no privacy, or do you want our own place?'

He waited, looking at her imploringly, then impatiently for an answer. May sat on the edge of the bed, staring blindly at her hands. Then slowly, grudgingly, she gave him the answer she would use over and over in the years to come, anything to avoid stirring his anger, anything to avoid creating conflict.

'I don't mind.'

✧ ✧ ✧

Over the next few weeks, the news became more and more sinister. Bert and Reggie would come back from the pub to the big house late at night now, wanting to talk about what they'd heard to the family, especially to Lydia.

Born after the end of the last war, both Stanley and May could see the fear in their faces, and the disbelief that it seemed to be happening all over again, despite what their father had fought for. Lydia couldn't remember the last war like Bert and Reggie could, but she did remember her father coming home. And how sad her mother had seemed to be all the time, even after he'd come home, especially after he'd come home.

The Sudetenland, the Rhineland. Rumours of the Jews fleeing Germany, of people disappearing in the night. Confusion and collective disbelief, after all, hadn't Chamberlain promised peace in Europe?

And then it happened.

Hitler invaded Poland.

The whole family gathered together to listen to the announcement on the wireless. Lydia sat, weeping quietly as war was declared, rocking back and forth on the edge of her chair and clutching May's icy hand, Bert and Reggie shoulder to shoulder, their faces set and grim. Jimmy standing removed with his back to the room, staring out of the window. And as the last words died away with the static of the wireless, Stanley stood up and, without a word, walked purposefully out of the door, leaving the little family stricken and silent.

He walked briskly round to Millie's, his mind clearer than it ever had been, his destiny now foreseen. When he raised his hand, the door opened before he could knock, Millie already waiting there with tears running down her face. Feeling his heart bursting

58

to see her distress, he gathered her to him and held her tight as she sobbed against his chest.

'What are you going to do?' she managed finally, pulling her tear-stained face away to look at him properly.

'I'm going to enlist,' he said brutally, to a new wave of sobbing. "I have to, you see Millie, if I don't, what was the point of my dad fighting in the last war? If we let the Germans do it again anyway?'

Millie seemed to struggle against him, then he realised that she was nodding, agreeing with him, although at what personal cost he could only guess.

'I know, Stanley, and I do understand, really I do,' she replied, her breath catching as she spoke. 'There's nothing to say that I have to like it though, is there?'

Feeling that her heart was breaking inside her, she gave him a watery smile, determined to show him that she would support and love him in this most momentous of decisions, and Stanley glowed with pride at the bravery he could see pasted across her white face.

'Millie, I want us to be married,' he blurted, his words surprising him, but in their utterance realising that they were what he had been wanting to say for a long time now.

Millie smiled properly now, her eyes glowing with sudden happiness.

'I've been hoping you'd ask me one day soon!' she laughed.

'So is it a "yes"?' he asked tentatively, and she rewarded him with a kiss that he would never forget.

'It's a "yes".'

Millie and Stanley broke their news to her mother, then to the subdued Johnson family later that day, then with the quiet accord that they had come to share, walked hand in hand to the church to ask for a special dispensation to marry quickly.

The vicar looked at them sadly, realising that many similar requests were about to come pouring through his doors. He advised Stanley that he would actually need proof that he had enlisted, and Stanley, anxious not to delay, left at run from the church gate to go and find out how to do this. The vicar stayed talking to Millie for a while, tactfully trying to discover if this was really what she wanted, this hasty wedding in such unsettled times. Looking at him sorrowfully, she drew a tremulous breath and answered directly and truthfully,

'Yes of course going to war has rushed us. But if it's for the rest of our lives, we might as well get started as soon as we can. I want him to know I'm here for him when he gets back.'

He looked at her appraisingly, admiring her bravery and honesty, and promised her he would move heaven and earth to get a quick wedding granted, and with that, she went home to make plans with her mother.

Stanley, meanwhile, had not found it difficult to discover how to enlist. Announcements were already cutting through the peaceful warmth of the September day from a loudspeaker outside the gates of Alexandra Palace, where a recruiting station had been hurriedly set up. The next few hours passed in a whirl of activity, which he passed through like a man in a daze. Uniform, boots, sign here. Report tomorrow morning at 8 o'clock, sharp.

He was unsurprised to meet Reggie and Bert there too, as well as Jimmy. All three had walked up as soon as he and Millie had left to speak to the vicar, so they already had their uniforms on, crisp, purposeful and incongruous in the hazy summer afternoon. They surveyed each other soberly, suddenly seeing themselves in a new light, a grown-up and harsh light, leaving no room for youth or inexperience.

'Anyone for a pint?' asked Reg quietly, and, without any further discussion, the four of them walked down the hill and into the pub, where Millie took one look at them in their uniform and at her new fiancé, and burst into tears all over again, tears both of fear and pride for the man she loved with all her heart.

And that night, the very first air raid warning rang out, splitting the night with its dreadful, alien, caterwauling howl. Reeling with shock and confusion, Jimmy, May, Lydia and Stanley stumbled into the kitchen, then out onto the street where all hell was breaking loose. Men in uniform were shouting at them, herding them back inside, 'Get into your shelters or get under the table!'

Terrified, May looked helplessly to Stanley for direction; they had not heeded the warnings over the past few weeks about preparing for this eventuality, like so many in London had chosen not to hear what was being said on the wireless. They looked at each other, faces stark with fear, then scrambled hastily under the table, jamming against each other out of necessity and also from an unacknowledged need for comfort until the all-clear finally sounded.

The next day dawned bright and beautiful, making the events of the long and terrible night seem like a bad dream. Jimmy and Stanley came down to the table in their stiff, unfamiliar uniforms, neither feeling able to face the food that Lydia and May had set on the table before them. Lydia looked at them anxiously.

'You really should eat, you don't know what the day will bring,' she said, and at that, Stanley put his hand to his mouth and bolted outside. Lydia looked at Jimmy, helplessly.

'Leave it, Lydia,' he said brusquely, 'I'll go.'

But as he got up to follow Stanley, May put her hand against his chest and stopped him, gently.

'No Jimmy, let me,' she said quietly, and stepping aside, he let her go after him.

Looking through the window, Lydia and Jimmy saw her stand beside him and put a hand onto his shuddering shoulders. A few moments passed, then Stanley turned and wrapped his arms gratefully around her, twin to twin locked in a silent embrace, needing no words. Then May looked up, caught Jimmy's eye through the window, and beckoned to him.

'Can you get your stuff,' she asked, urgently, 'yours and his?'

Jimmy nodded and joined them again a few moments later. As Stanley pulled away from May, Jimmy leant over and gave her a quick, hard kiss, then he and Stanley left without a word, walking up the hill together side by side.

Lydia scraped the untouched food into the bin, then sat at the table, put her face in her hands, and wept the complicated tears both of a sister and a surrogate mother suddenly bereft of her charges.

Millie left for work early, intending to scrub the bar spotless, hoping to blot out her fears. Hoping against hope that Stanley would not be sent away too far, too soon.

May left for work without going back into the house, unable to face Lydia's grief with her own as she watched her twin brother walk away, and unwilling to allow her to see her relief that Jimmy had gone too. As her husband went off to face a new and uncertain future, she sat calmly at her machine, the needle flying fast and the material guided instinctively by her increasingly deft hands. The whirring of the machine and the song in her heart brought a glowing smile to her face, and Janie, looking up and catching her unawares, caught her breath at the beauty in her features, shining through as if May was emerging from a dark chrysalis to spread her wings for the first time in the bright sunlight of a new day.

After the boys had left, Lydia sat at the kitchen table, stunned by the silence disturbed only by the ticking of the clock on the mantelpiece. Her tearful vigil was abruptly disturbed by the sound of knocking at the back door. Surprised, she wiped her eyes, straightened her apron, and went to the door, wondering who could be calling during this strange day.

She caught her breath when she saw it was Arthur – and with her in such a state! Hastily, she pushed back her dishevelled hair, and looked up at him enquiringly as he pushed through the door, puzzled by his lack of greeting. Then she looked at him properly, and realised he was unable to speak, struggling with an emotion so powerful it was rendering him incapable. Quietly, she waited for him to gather himself, to regain control, afraid of what he was going to say.

'I tried to enlist, he gasped eventually, 'I tried to volunteer, but Lydia, they wouldn't have me!'

His cry of anguish resounded through the silent kitchen, and gently, she gathered him against her, rocking him like she used to do with May when she was little, back in the days when she could still help her.

Word by painful word, Arthur's story emerged. Just like everyone else, he had gone to sign up with his friends, determined to do his bit, determined to volunteer and fight together. But, apparently, the powers that be had a list of 'protected' occupations, occupations deemed so important that those individuals could not be spared to risk their lives for King and Country. Being a railway worker was one of those occupations, so it would seem, and Arthur, being in the senior position of Station Master, was not at liberty to offer himself elsewhere.

At any price.

Arthur sat staring at his hands, his emotion spent, unable to meet Lydia's eye.

'What are they going to say?' he mumbled brokenly under his breath. 'What are your brothers going to think of me?'

Lydia stared at him silently, appalled. Trying desperately to marshal her thoughts, to find some words of comfort for her man sitting devastated before her. To her shame, she realised that in truth she was torn in two, part of her rejoicing that he wouldn't be sent away, that he would not be in danger, and partly crawling with the same shame that he was already suffering, that her man was somehow diminished by not being able to serve, to fight for her and for his country.

She swallowed hard and opened her arms to him. He leant into her embrace, and over his head she shut her eyes and offered a silent prayer that they would all come out of this unharmed.

By the end of that day, the men had been assigned to regiments, none of them the same due to the lessons learned from the Great War, when whole families, entire populations were wiped out in the same action, leaving no young men to return to their home town.

Stanley did not go straight home that night, turning his weary footsteps towards the pub to see Millie, whom he knew would be waiting anxiously for news. He walked through the door which banged behind him, making the young woman standing with her back to him start violently.

'I'm so sorry,' he blurted out, stricken by the sight of the white, tense face she turned towards him.

Millie's eyes filled with tears, but she brushed them away impatiently with the backs of her hands.

'So what's the verdict, then?' she asked, with the quiet fortitude he had come to love so well.

Stanley drew a deep breath, then took both her hands in his.

'Training camp begins in a week,' he replied softly, 'I'm not sure where exactly but I think it'll probably be in Kent, that's what the officers are saying today, anyway.'

'And then?' she asked, hardly daring to meet his eye.

'No one's saying, love,' he answered honestly, 'but I expect it will be France.'

Millie drew a long, shaky breath. 'Do you still think we can still get married first?' she asked, and Stanley grinned at her and caught her to his chest for a long moment.

'Let's go back to the vicar and ask what he's done with our special licence right now, shall we?'

And all of a sudden, Millie felt herself giving way to a tumult of emotion and let herself weep, finally, in the arms of the man she had come to love so much and now feared she might lose before the best had even had a chance to begin.

Stanley and Millie were married three days later in a poignant ceremony at the church where May and Jimmy had married in the spring. A rushed arrangement, a turmoil of emotion. The love for her young husband and pride in his decision battling in Millie's face with fear and grief as she walked up the aisle towards him, and as he turned to her and repeated the well-worn, time-honoured words of love, she could see her feelings reflected in his overly bright eyes.

May stood stiffly next to Jimmy, watching Millie leaning forward to say her marriage vows urgently and fervently almost as if she were in a private space with Stanley and no one there to watch. She had lent Millie her own wedding dress, although she had secretly had to repair a tear across the bodice, disguising the trauma and violence of her own wedding night with a minutely embroidered swathe of new lace, concealing it as effectively as she had the rift in her marriage. She watched enviously as her twin and friend kissed, wishing them luck and joy in her heart, hoping that they could find a moment of peace together before Stanley had to go. She marvelled at the irony of the scene – such a rushed wedding, the groom in uniform about to depart for war, yet both happy and radiant with the surety of their love. The comparison to her own situation was almost too painful to contemplate: the perfect courtship, the perfect wedding, yet she had to admit to herself, if to no one else, that she was profoundly relieved that Jimmy would be leaving the country imminently. She crossed her fingers behind her back then, shocked at her own thoughts, and suddenly feeling exposed as the kindly, gentle eyes of the vicar fell on her as he blessed all the boys, the children of the last war, heading off to the horrors he knew lay ahead of them.

Later, they all returned to the big house, trying feverishly to recreate the gaiety that anybody could wish for on their wedding day. Millie and Stanley pushed back the chairs in the front room and began to dance as Bert struck up a tune in time-honoured family tradition on his battered accordion, and Jimmy glanced at May and smiled encouragingly. She stood up and stretched out her hands to him, loving the feel of their closeness while they danced, the deep, unspoken connection that meant they danced in perfect harmony, their bodies blending together and seamlessly with the

music. She closed her eyes tightly, trying to hold on to u..
ment, trying not to let her mind wander to thoughts of the othe.
Jimmy, the Jimmy who seemed possessed by his own demons,
who frightened her out of her mind. He was not present today,
though, and like Millie, she let herself be caught up by the all-
encompassing love surrounding them, surrendered to the beauty
of the music, and danced.

The day they all left, the girls vowed they would go up to the
station together. The men breakfasted with them all together,
subdued by the enormity of their impending departure. Halfway
through breakfast though, May stood up suddenly, then swayed as
her face drained of all colour and began to cry bitterly, tears rolling unchecked down her face. Alarmed, Jimmy leapt to his feet
and put a steadying arm around her, and she smiled at him weakly
before sitting down again, looking sheepishly around the table as
she apologised for her behaviour. Lydia watched her closely, but
May caught her eye and shook her head sharply, dismissively. Lydia
let out her breath and looked away, her eyes smarting with the effort of staying in control. Arthur would be up at the station, she
knew, his feelings raw as he prepared to send the first recruits off
to a war he could not fight.

In the end, it all passed in such a rush there was little time to
feel the emotion that would hit them all later as they began to
understand the enormity of their actions.

Jimmy held May tightly and kissed her passionately on the lips,
barely registering her cooler response. He never seemed to notice her feelings, thought May bitterly, then forced her traitorous
thoughts out of her mind and made herself kiss him back fervently. Her husband was off to train to be a soldier, to fight the

Germans and protect her, the least she could do was to send him off with a kiss.

As Stanley released Millie, he turned to Lydia and May and gave them a tight smile.

'Look after my girl for me,' he managed, then gathered them both into a hard hug, releasing them abruptly to leap swiftly up from the platform to join Reggie and Bert on the waiting train. As the train pulled away from the station, women young and old waved their hankies in a flurry, waving off their young men to war.

And Lydia, catching a glimpse of Arthur, standing silently and utterly alone with his flag in his Station Master's uniform, pretended not to see him, ashamedly ducked her head and turned her face away in a flurry of confusion, relief and shame.

The next day dawned clear and bright, and all seemed terribly normal, except for the quietness of the house. 'I think we should ask Millie if her mum would like to move in for a bit,' said Lydia thoughtfully over their very sombre breakfast, the two of them trying to act as if all was well. May nodded firmly.

'We've got plenty of space,' she agreed, 'but I think we should probably wait 'til the boys are back from training before we say anything, we don't want to make any big decisions when we don't know how long this is all going to go on.'

Lydia sat in agreement, both of them weighed down by the thought of their brothers going off to unimaginable places to fight, neither girl had ever travelled further than Southend before and the enormity of the situation loomed over them menacingly.

All of a sudden, May leapt to her feet, and just like the day before, went white as a sheet. Lydia looked at her in alarm and went to get up, but May had already bolted through the kitchen door to the little privy out the back. Lydia followed her more slowly, then heard her vomiting painfully and froze, appalled, her thoughts rushing back to unwanted memories of her mother staggering out day after day to be sick, just like this. Then she had died and left them, but the screams from that terrible night and her father's destroyed face had never left her and now reverberated through her mind.

'May?' she asked, tentatively, then stepped back as the privy door swung open. May stood leaning against the door frame, ashen-faced.

'I think I need to see a doctor,' she confessed, shakily, 'I've been feeling sick these last few days, but I thought I was just worried about the boys. I feel so bad today though, Lydia, maybe I should see if something's really wrong.'

Lydia gazed at her, silently marvelling at the depths of her innocence, while at the same time, trying to ignore a nagging feeling of guilt. Her role of mother to the family had never sat easily on her young shoulders, and she had never really talked to May about growing up, had just hoped May would find out for herself without having to discuss all the details about which she still found herself utterly unfamiliar.

She pulled herself together, realising then that she needed to help May accept her new responsibility, her new role.

'Come and sit down, May,' she said kindly, and led her gently by the hand back into the kitchen, 'I've got something exciting to tell you.'

Janie looked across at the face of her friend later that day, and was shocked to see how pale she was. No wonder, she thought to herself sadly, with that gorgeous new husband of hers going off to be a soldier, May must be feeling awful.

May felt the weight of Janie's gaze, looked up and caught her eye. She smiled wanly, then got on with her work, the needle whirring hypnotically and allowing her mind to switch off from the terrifying thoughts that were threatening to consume her. She was becoming adept at blocking painful thoughts, after all, she had had plenty of practice in her short marriage.

Janie was not the only one watching May this morning. Just before Janie and May were going off for their lunch-break, they were called over to the big desk by Mr Courtney, who looked them over appraisingly.

'You two are doing fine work there,' he said to them cheerily, 'but I wondered if you'd like to try something a little different today?'

May smiled at him, she liked her new boss, he was quick to praise and generous with it. She had never earned so much before, but more importantly, he valued her work and made her feel appreciated, which her fragile self-esteem needed desperately.

It transpired that two of the girls who worked out front in the very swanky shop had not turned up for work today. Mr Courtney had an important client coming to view his new collection, and he urgently needed models. With May's tiny, hourglass figure and Janie's slender willowy shape, the two of them were just what he needed to save the day, and he kicked himself for not realising it sooner, thanking his lucky stars that his desk, deliberately placed to help him keep an eye on the factory floor, had allowed his eyes to rest on precisely what he was looking for.

Janie and May couldn't believe their eyes when they were shown through the door marked 'private' and into another world, a world away from the whirr of the machines and the chatter of the factory.

The shop front itself was draped in grey silk, and centre stage was a single creation that drew the eye with its simple elegance, a red crepe dress falling in soft folds over the figure of the manikin beneath.

May glanced round swiftly, her imagination caught by the simplicity of the design of the dress, and awed by the wealth exuding from the austere but classic shop frontage. Her reverie was suddenly interrupted, however, by the bustling arrival of a plump, cheerful lady, Mrs Hargreaves, who briskly ran her practised eye over their figures as Mr Courtney had done just a few moments earlier.

'Perfect,' she muttered to herself, then smiling, she ushered them through to a large changing area, full of bright lights and mirrors. 'I'll measure you both first,' she said, 'just strip down to your bra and pants and we'll get started.'

Janie grinned at May's aghast expression.

'It's all girls together,' she laughed encouragingly, and promptly slipped off her blouse and skirt and stood obligingly with her arms outstretched before Mrs Hargreaves.

'I'm sorry,' May burst out, horrified, 'I just can't!' She could feel the tears welling up behind her eyes and swallowed hard. Mrs Hargreaves looked at her sympathetically, then said firmly,

'We really need you May, the first time is always a bit nerve-wracking, but believe me, I've seen it all before!' She waited expectantly, then sighed as May stood still, transfixed with horror.

'Come on May,' said Janie, moved by her friend's apparent plight. She looked at Mrs Hargreaves and glanced fractionally at the door, the older woman understood and made to leave, recognising that Janie was perhaps more adept at this than she was.

Janie took May's hand and made her look up at her.

'Come on, May,' she said again, more firmly this time, 'you know how much Mr Courtney needs this, he wouldn't ask if he wasn't desperate!'

May took a long, ragged breath, then nodded. Janie squeezed her hand tightly, then released it so that May could undo her buttons and slip her blouse off her shoulders.

And as she did so, Janie caught her breath as she saw May's back reflected in the mirror behind, the weals and scars of her beatings exposed in the harsh white lights overhead. Then looked at her friend who stood with her chin up, her eyes flashing a warning. Defying Janie to comment, daring her to sympathise, refusing to acknowledge what she knew Janie must have seen.

And when Mrs Hargreaves walked discreetly back through the door carrying an armful of clothes, all three women carried on as normal, as if oblivious to the evidence of violence displayed so brutally and oh, so blatantly before their eyes.

The two weeks of training camp passed swiftly, much too swiftly for May, who had little time to gather her emotions over the news with which her sister Lydia had enlightened her.

Burdened her.

A baby. Jimmy's baby, and a war on too. She sighed heavily each time she contemplated the reality of her situation, she had absolutely no idea how Jimmy would take the news. Lydia had been so sweet, and very kind and considerate bringing her toast to her room each morning so she didn't feel quite so sick.

May hadn't meant to tell her, but Millie had guessed immediately that first day after the boys had left, the three of them sitting in unaccustomed silence as they readjusted to the echoing emptiness of the big house. May's hand had inadvertently strayed, as every newly expectant mother's does, to touch and protect the unborn baby within, cradling her stomach with fierce and instinctive pride. Millie's perceptive eyes had spotted it at once, she had been excited, clearly moved.

'You're so lucky,' she'd whispered as she'd hugged her new sister-in-law, 'at least you have something of Jimmy's to keep you company, I wish I was having Stanley's baby!' Then she had burst into tears and they had all sat, laughing and crying and hugging each other in an outpouring of emotion that had been waiting to erupt since they'd waved off the train.

Arthur knocked on the door then, and Millie and May had made themselves scarce, one look at Lydia's stricken, guilty face was enough to know that they needed to be alone.

Arthur crossed the room in three strides and put his arms out to Lydia, who looked away, unable to marshal her feelings.

'Lydia, look at me,' he demanded quietly, and when she did not, he put his fingers gently under her chin and tilted her face up to his, the intensity of his gaze making her cheeks burn.

'Lydia,' he began again, faltering a little this time, but determined to have his say, 'I love you, Lyd. I wish I could've gone too, but I can't, and that's all there is to it! At least I tried to volunteer!'

His last words came out too loudly and made Lydia jump, helped her focus on how she really felt. She looked at Arthur, at his kind, strong face, and knew deep inside, recognised finally that she truly loved him.

'I'm so sorry,' she blurted, but he stopped her with a hard kiss.

'No need to be sorry, sweetheart.'

'But yes there is,' she said desperately, trying to meet his eye but wanting to hide her face at the same time, 'I saw you at the station and I cut you dead, I pretended I hadn't seen you, I felt so awful with everyone leaving and I didn't know what to say,' she wailed miserably, then burst into hot tears of shame and turned her head away again.

Then, through her tears, she heard a tiny, hard laugh, and looked up to see Arthur trying valiantly to smile.

'I guess I'd better get used to it,' he managed, 'and Lydia, I saw you look away yesterday. I understand, honestly I do, I've been struggling with this too, remember, they're my friends too and I wanted to fight alongside them!'

Lydia lifted her face to him and smiled at him tremulously, wishing she could atone for her behaviour and wanting more than anything to make Arthur feel better. She kissed him tentatively, then harder as he kissed her back, and it seemed the most natural thing in the world to lead him upstairs into her bedroom and find solace in each other's bodies, the two of them united together against the mad world outside.

May straightened her dress one last time, then smiled nervously at herself in the tiny cracked mirror, before running downstairs to join Lydia and Millie. The three of them hugged wordlessly, then left to walk up the hill towards the station. The train was pulling in when they arrived, and as Arthur raised his flag, he looked directly at Lydia, and May could have sworn that he had winked.

Jimmy was first off the train, sweeping May up in an extravagance of affection, kissing her on the lips in front of them all. Stanley, Bert and Reggie were quick on his heels, all of them chattering loudly, making the girls realise how contracted and just how quiet their world had become in the two short weeks without them.

Stanley and Millie walked off together without a backwards glance, straight towards their favourite place, Alexandra Palace gardens, without even needing to suggest it to each other, tacit in their mutual understanding.

Lydia fussed around her brothers in the kitchen, and all too soon, May ran out of excuses and found herself in the bedroom, alone with Jimmy.

He kissed her passionately, pushing her back towards the bed, groaned in her ear,

'God I've missed you, May, I've missed you so much!'

As she fell backwards in his embrace her hands again went instinctively and protectively to her stomach, and he pulled away suddenly, staring at her in amazement and disbelief. She had to laugh then, his face was a comic picture, and all of a sudden everything was all right, her Jimmy was like a dog with a bone, delightedly undoing her dress to lie his head adoringly against her still flat stomach.

It was everything she could have hoped for. The next few days, Jimmy was loving and solicitous, but best of all, he was proud. He paraded May around their friends and family, beaming all over his face every time he caught her eye. May felt bathed in glory, delighted by his attention, and it was clear to everyone who saw her that she was glowing with his love.

Janie watched her like a hawk at work. Nothing had been said, nothing acknowledged. Sometimes she felt that the secret lay between them, but in reality, May seemed to have simply filed it away, refusing to allow Janie a chance to even comment on what she had surely seen. Now Janie was confused, she had been introduced to Jimmy who seemed such a lovely, gentle man, clearly in love with his wife and excited by the prospect of becoming a father. Was it definitely him who had hurt May? Had Janie misinterpreted what she had seen?

She sighed to herself, wishing her new friend wasn't quite so proud, so intensely loyal. She would just have to wait until May asked for her help, though how bad it would have to get beyond what she had already witnessed flayed across her poor back, God forbid.

When they left, they left for France. The news was positive, the war would be over and the boys home by Christmas. The atmosphere at the station was buoyant, the girls tearful but smiling as they waved off their loved ones once again. As he hugged her, Jimmy put his hand over May's belly almost reverently, whispered loving words in her ear about seeing a 'proper bump' when he got back.

'Look after yourself, the both of you!' he said quietly, his words catching suddenly in his throat. May kissed him impulsively, hoping for a new beginning, daring to believe that her Jimmy had changed now that she was becoming a mother.

A new routine developed in the big house. Millie's mother was often around for a spot of company but didn't elect to move in, preferring the girls to visit her in her own home. Millie, Lydia and May spent most afternoons together after May got home from work, sharing a quick pot of tea before Millie went off to her shift at the pub, Arthur joining them when his work allowed.

Days stretched to weeks, weeks with no word from France, except the news on the wireless saying the boys were doing well, that the Germans were being thwarted, that the boys were winning the day.

And then Christmas came and went, Millie's mum joining them for a subdued, sad meal, the absence of the boys weighing increasingly heavily on them all. The war seemed so remote, unconnected to what seemed to be their normal lives, normal except for the absence of the country's young men.

The advent of rationing came as a sudden shock, bringing it home to them for the first time that this war might not be short. Might not have an end in sight after all. The first fear began to grip London, spreading across the country like an infection.

Lydia learned to queue with their ration books, thanking her lucky stars that May could get extra as she was expecting and was happy to share her little bonuses with the family. The winter became colder, the news more bleak. No swift victory, no returning heroes.

Then one night, Lydia was woken by the sound of insistent banging on the back door, hammering almost as hard as her frightened heart. She ran to open up the door, then paused for a moment, terrified of what news might be delivered by her night time visitor.

It was Arthur. Ashen but calm, rushed but authoritative.

'I need you to put the word out in the street,' he said briskly. 'There's been a battle and the boys are being brought back, tonight. I need you all to come and help them off the train, get them home.'

Lydia stared at him, uncomprehendingly.

'All of them?' she asked, dazedly.

Arthur grimaced, only too aware that Lydia had three brothers and her brother-in-law out there somewhere, their backs to the sea and awaiting rescue in a rout of such epic proportion the country would shudder to recall it.

'All of them.'

It went on for more hours than they could bear to remember. Back and forth to the station as the trains rolled in one after another, hour after hour expelling soaking, stinking, bloody men, men staggering with exhaustion and weak with defeat. London's women arrived to meet them, no longer looking for their own in the chaos and confusion, all just reaching out, as one soul to another, to give succour to anyone they could.

And on the other side of the channel, in the cold light of dawn, the queues of men stretched out into the sea, waiting their turn for a boat, held upright by the best of British discipline and the best of human courage.

Stanley stood, ice-cold and waist-deep, supporting another unknown soldier who could barely stand. The man was an officer, and had taken a wound through his hip; in the dim light Stanley could see the blood spreading like a dirty stain into the water in the half light of the morning. At last, another boat came into view, picking its way carefully through the waves towards the line of waiting men. In unison, they surged forward, grasping frantically towards the gunnels, inadvertently half-swamping the little yacht in their desperation, then a cry of anguish dragged from parched throats as the boat turned sharply out to sea again as a wave of bullets whined overhead. Men dropped and slid beneath the waves. The queue closed up on itself, a new surge towards the boat which had gallantly turned towards them again.

The officer stirred, pulled himself up on Stanley and wrapped his arm around his shoulders in his determination to stay upright.

'Stay back!' he barked. 'If you swamp him we're all lost. One by one, men!'

The sense of the order permeated through the shattered men, and they formed a line again as best they could in the icy waves, filing towards the boat in quiet discipline.

Stanley tried to step forward with the officer, but the weight of his increasingly limp body weighed him down. He shrugged off his backpack with difficulty, hearing the words of the sergeant at training camp an eternity ago, yet ringing remorselessly in his ears on this terrible day: 'Never, ever, dump your equipment, it is not yours to dump, it is the Army's!' He surged forwards at last, and the officer groaned, opened his eyes, then jerked his head up, staring at Stanley as if he were seeing a ghost.

'What's your name, Private?' he asked, wincing with the effort of speaking through his chapped and bleeding lips.

'Johnson, Stanley Johnson,' replied Stanley, and watched as the older man gave a nod, a start of recognition, then sagged a little lower into the water.

'Do I know you?' he asked in confusion.

The officer grimaced and tried to smile.

'Such a family likeness,' he whispered. 'That black hair. I believe you must be related to Edie Johnson, but you may be too young, it was a long time ago.'

Stanley heard the name with a shudder of recognition, Edie, the older sister he and May had never known. He had been brought up with the tragic story of her loss, and the young soldier, then a sergeant, who was to have married her after surviving the Great War. He nodded, then watched the officer's eyes fill with sudden tears.

'She was my fiancée,' he managed, painfully, his breath rasping in his throat.

Stanley stared at him, disbelievingly, unable to comprehend the hand of fate that could mean that all these years later, he could be supporting his once-to-be brother-in-law above the surface of an icy sea as they tried to flee back to the country they were fighting for together, for Edward Peters' second time.

There was nothing more to be said. Stanley hoisted Edward as high as he could, and pushed determinedly towards the boat.

When his turn finally came, he struggled to lift the weight of his officer, his brother that never was, imploring the man on the boat to take them both, to help him lift his limp but precious cargo aboard. Not understanding the kindly but insistent hands prising his fingers away from the wet coarseness of Edward's jacket, not recognising the guttural sounds of harsh weeping as his own as they gently but firmly slipped the lifeless body back under the sucking, hungry pull of the tide.

All the boys came home.

One by one, some on the same train, some not, they all came home in dribs and drabs. Jimmy, Bert, Reggie and Stanley, all helped off the train by Arthur, all helped down to the big house by their waiting women, shocked by the naked grief and exhaustion etched on their young faces.

And, like their forefathers before them, unable to share their experiences, unwilling to taint their homes with the horror that they had just endured.

All except Stanley, whose other talent for communication unwittingly made the connection, the missing link between the girls and their men in those few, strained days, bridged the gap between those who were there and those who were not.

Millie came awake in the night, lay there listening quietly as she struggled to understand what had woken her. A sound she had heard but a few times in the brief days of her marriage, but many, many times in their intimate courtship, the sounds of pencil on paper, committing memory to tangible contour, thought to form.

She slipped noiselessly from the bed, padded softly over to where Stanley sat in the harsh glare of the little gas light. What she saw made her catch her breath in horror, in sympathy and despair. Lines upon lines of men, stretching out into the sea. Plucky little boats – such little boats! – working their precarious way through the mudbanks to meet them, bravely risking all to drag more souls away from the enemy and from the sea. And all the time, relentless fire overhead, bullets whining, shells exploding. Bodies floating.

All that could not be conveyed was the sound, the noise of attack, retreat, survival, defeat. Even so, the raw horror of the scene impressed itself upon Millie's appalled eyes, and in that moment, she suddenly understood, finally recognised with terrifying clarity, the time-honoured role of the soldier's wife. To support. To provide a home, free from fear, free from violence. A home full of compassion, space to talk, but devoid of demands, of questions. A place to nurture and heal, a place to dream. Just as Edie had once dreamed of after the war she thought Edward had won.

She touched Stanley lightly on the shoulder, felt him recoil, then relax slowly, leaning back with a deep, shuddering sigh against her waiting body. Then she took his hand and led him back to their cold bed, warmed him with her body and held him silently while he wept.

The next day, he told them about Edward. He sat at the breakfast table in the grey light of a London morning and told his tale compulsively, torn from him in word by agonised word, his family beleaguered by the story that he uttered, scarcely unable to tolerate much more pain, more loss. Lydia, besieged by the memories of her beautiful yet dimly recalled big sister, May, struck dumb by the shared misery of the collective family memory which, until now, she had been too young to share. Bert and Reggie, much older, struggling to contain their emotion, both looking down at the scrubbed table top and blinking away bitter, shaming tears.

And in that moment of shared grief, Millie, Arthur and Jimmy finally found common ground, working together to help the diminished, stricken little family. Nothing clever, nothing fancy, just tea, porridge, gently moving May out of the door and off to work, putting the kitchen to rights while the older siblings sat quietly, gathering strength from one another, from being home.

Small comfort indeed.

That day, Janie kept glancing across at May, noticing each time she leant back to rub her aching back, the cheap fabric of her maternity smock stretching across her breasts. She caught her eye, smiled sympathetically, then stood up in alarm as she saw her friend's eyes filling with ready tears. She glanced quickly aside at Mr Courtney, whose watchful eye as usual had missed nothing. He nodded briefly but firmly, then looked away as Janie took May's trembling hand and led her out the back to the little yard behind the factory.

Tiredly, May leaned back against the soot-stained wall, uncaring about the mess it would make of her pretty, painstakingly stitched outfit that the two of them had made out of cast-offs discreetly donated by their kindly boss, sitting giggling late into the evening and swapping confidences about their homes, their lives, their men. Up to a point, the point when May's face would close like a shutter caught in the wind, clipping the conversation to an untimely end. Time and time again. Janie despaired of ever encouraging her to open up, to tell her the truth behind her oh-so-perfect husband.

'All right?' Janie ventured, at last.

May sighed, opened her eyes and looked at her friend.

'He's home,' she said, quietly. 'Jimmy's home.'

Janie gazed at her, uncertainly.

'Is he hurt?' she asked, suddenly afraid where the conversation might lead.

May laughed, then,

'No,' she answered harshly, 'no, he's not hurt.' She stopped, checked herself before she said more. Before she told Janie that she was afraid to go home, that she was afraid to be alone with him. Afraid for the baby. That she wished he hadn't come back. She shook her head, furiously, denying herself the right to think the unthinkable.

Her soldier boy was home and now it was her turn to do her duty.

That night, she lay, face to face with Jimmy in their narrow bunks in the Anderson shelter that Lydia had had built a few weeks before, silently listening to the destruction overhead and desperately willing it to stop. Just before dawn, it all went quiet, and May awoke suddenly, uncomfortably aware of being watched. Jimmy hadn't moved, was still gazing at her across the narrow divide. He reached out his hand and rested it reverently on her bump, caught her eye and gave her a complicit grin when the baby gave an answering kick.

'I want you out of here,' he mouthed, then repeated more firmly, 'I want you out of here, May, you and the baby.'

She nodded, mutely. She had known this was coming, had expected it from the moment that the men realised they were sleeping in the shelter every night, and she almost felt relieved. Then she thought of Lydia's solid support, of Millie's ready friendship, and her heart twisted sharply with fear and impending loneliness.

What did she know about having a baby, she hadn't even known how she'd fallen pregnant, she'd needed her big sister to enlighten her! She bit her lip hard to stop it trembling, and forced herself to give Jimmy what he wanted to see, a bright, brittle smile.

'I can get evacuated next week, they said,' she confessed. 'All pregnant women can go if they want to.'

Jimmy's troubled face cleared.

'It's best, May,' he declared, 'then you can get used to the baby and soon we can be a proper family, just the three of us, just as soon as all this is over.'

The boys were called back up over the next few days, each heading off separately this time to their own regiments. Millie took it harder this time, she who had grown so close to Stanley, had shared his intimate portrayal of the 'success' of Dunkirk and now understood much more than she ever wanted to of the dangers they faced.

The girls clung together mentally for support in those dark days, Millie consumed by her own, very graphic fears, May with her immediate worries about her impending delivery and the safety of her unborn baby. And Lydia watched them both, finally realising how lucky she was to have Arthur safe and close by, drawing comfort and courage from his strength and the quiet dignity of his presence. And holding onto a newfound pride in his steadfastness and strength on the night of the evacuation, when he had mobilised the women of Muswell Hill to look after their own and anyone else they could reach out to.

The day before May was evacuated stood out in her mind as the worst night of bombing that she could remember. As she picked her way gingerly through the smoke and rubble to work that day, she turned her face away from the dusty destruction all about her and the imperative commands of the ARP wardens as they tried to organise the chaos around them. Like every pregnant woman before her, she spread her hands protectively across her bump, as if this tiny, futile gesture could protect her unborn baby from the horror surrounding her.

When the factory clock chimed five, May pushed back her chair and looked speechlessly at Janie sitting opposite as always, suddenly overwhelmed by the emotions flooding through her at the thought of leaving. Looking at her friend tremulously, only now did she truly realise just how much she had grown to love working there.

'Behind you,' hissed Janie suddenly, and May turned to see Mr Courtney walking over with carrying a large bag.

'A present for the baby,' he said, looking rather uncomfortable as he handed over the bag, and May was astonished to see that it was full of baby clothes.

'Mrs Hargreaves helped me get them together for you,' he explained self-consciously, and May looked at him with a lump in her throat, knowing just how much she owed him for taking a chance on her when he gave her a job.

'I'll come back to work after the baby,' she burst out impetuously, and Mr Courtney smiled at her tenderly, knowing that he was unlikely to see her again, given the circumstances.

'When you're ready, May,' he said gruffly, and turned away, hastily.

Janie gave her a sympathetic grin when she saw her swallowing back her tears.

'He's nice, he is,' she offered.

May gave her a shaky smile, and suddenly they were hugging each other and crying properly now.

'You'll write and tell me where you are?' demanded Janie for the umpteenth time.

'Of course I will,' said May, pulling away to give her a watery smile. 'And you stay safe, now,' she added sharply, and Janie rolled her eyes and nodded sheepishly, May had railed against her about ignoring the air raid sirens and determinedly sleeping through, her only protection from the Luftwaffe's worst being a pillow over her head to block out the whining of the dropping bombs.

'I'll go the shelter,' she smiled, 'but I hate to give Hitler the satisfaction of really disturbing me!'

Their tears turned to wry laughter at the thought that Hitler could disturb them any further than he already had, and May squeezed Janie close as they kissed goodbye, the loss of the easy laughter she always shared with her precious friend suddenly seeming almost too hard to bear.

May was to catch the train at eight the next morning, with the instruction to take the minimum of luggage, just one small trunk to see her through 'until it was over'.

Lydia had knocked on her bedroom door that evening, just as she was packing the last of the new baby clothes into the battered trunk Arthur had acquired for her. She came hesitantly into the room she had not entered since May's marriage, looked at her little sister and caught her breath when she saw May sitting on the bed with tears rolling down her face, unchecked. Lydia went straight to her, wrapped her in her arms and held her, feeling the baby jump between them as she rocked her like she had when she was a child and first began taking the tentative steps to being mother and carer to her orphaned family.

May drew a deep, shuddering breath then pulled away to look at Lydia, wiping her tears with the back of her hand, the likeness to the child she had once been belied by the grim expression behind her eyes.

'I'm just being silly,' she said, tiredly. 'It's been quite a day, leaving work and everything. And now packing to go, I've never been anywhere and I'm so afraid, Lydia.'

Her simple words caught Lydia's heart, and she bit back her own tears as always to help her sister.

'You'll be all right, May,' she said, more firmly than she felt. 'You're going to be such a good mother, you'll see!'

May looked at her and began to shake her head, tears beginning to fall again despite all her efforts to stop them.

'I don't know the first thing about babies,' she said helplessly. 'I didn't even know how I made this one! I don't know how to hold one, how to nurse one, I don't know anything, Lydia!'

Lydia smiled and hugged her hard. 'You'll do what every other mother has always done, since the beginning of time, May,' she said with conviction. 'You'll learn as it happens, you'll ask other mothers, you'll get help when you need it from the midwives, they'll be brilliant, you'll see!'

'Will you come with me to the station?' asked May, quietly. Lydia nodded, not trusting herself to speak now, willing herself to stay strong for May.

'What about you and Arthur?' May asked, suddenly, catching Lydia off guard with her unexpected question. 'I know you two are seeing each other,' insisted May, 'and I know it's serious between you.'

Lydia smiled, suddenly glad to be sharing her confidence with her sister.

'We've been seeing rather too much of each other lately,' she confessed, and May blushed when she caught her meaning. She looked at Lydia questioningly, and she smiled again.

'It makes it all seem crazy, this war,' she began, slowly. 'Sometimes you look at what's important, getting married, not getting married, having babies, worrying about what people think, when just over the Channel our brothers are shooting people, trying not to get shot themselves. I expect we'll get married soon, maybe, maybe not. But we don't want any fuss, it seems wrong with what's happening out there.'

It was May's turn to hug Lydia now. The eldest and youngest held each other close for a long and tender moment, painfully aware that the next day they would need to find the strength to face the next hurdle of their lives alone.

Millie arrived home, much to her surprise, to a silent and apparently empty house.

'Lydia?' she called, uncertainly, as she took in the deserted kitchen with no sign of her sister-in-law's presence nor dinner on the stove. She listened for a moment at the bottom of the stairs, then heard the murmur of low voices coming from the direction of May's closed door.

'May?' she called, more loudly now, afraid to intrude but also alarmed by the uncharacteristic lack of bustle to which they had all grown accustomed, the three of them working alongside to retain the sense of normality they all so desperately craved. She jumped as the bedroom door clicked open on the landing, and Lydia smiled down at her through the tears on her face.

'Oh Lydia,' Millie burst out, and took the stairs at an indecorous two at a time to give Lydia a hug, feeling her trembling against her as she tried to control her sobs. 'And May, you're not much better, are you,' she observed wryly, pushing the door wide and, catching her eye, May began to giggle though her tears, and soon all three of them were clutching at each other, laughing and crying as they held one another.

'Right,' said Millie firmly, looking around at them as they all finally began to calm down, 'I think we need a night out to see May off.'

The sisters looked at her, blankly.

'The pub!' she laughed, their bemused faces making the mirth rise up within her again. 'It's not just for the boys, you know!'

In a way, she was wrong. It always had been just the boys, Lydia and May forever watching as their brothers left with Dad. It had never been a place that they would have thought to frequent and had not been part of their life as a family. Giving herself a shake, Lydia was the first to pull herself together.

'You're right,' she said, impishly, 'after all there *is* a war on!'

And with that, the three of them buckled on their best shoes and walked arm in arm up Muswell Hill to the pub where Millie worked, taking in the noise and chatter as they entered coming from the older men and others left behind. Lydia spotted Arthur at once, and he joined them immediately, raising his eyebrows quizzically at them as they went to get a table.

'Drink, ladies?' he asked mischievously, and within a moment, the four of them were sitting companionably nursing port and lemon, May and Lydia's shoulders touching gently as they sat closer than they had been for years.

And when the piano struck up a tune, it seemed the most natural thing in the world for them to gather around together, Lydia's high, sweet voice soaring up with the melody while Arthur, May and Millie listened, arms around each other's waists, the simple pleasure of company and music filling them with the comfort and joy that can only come from being with the closest of family and friends. And later that night, the girls all hugged and kissed in the kitchen, savouring that last precious evening and promising they would all do it again as soon as they were all back, all of them home and together again after the war was over.

Part Four

1940, Evacuation

May got off the train, as instructed, in Hitchin, Hertfordshire, clutching her bag to her chest and waiting for the porter to pass her trunk down onto the crowded platform.

She looked around uncertainly, then resignedly joined the back of a queue of children standing by a lady with a clipboard and pencil, tiredly scanning her list and calling out names. Some of the children were crying, and all of them looked afraid.

'I don't want two of them,' insisted a harassed and irritable-looking lady, 'I said I only have space for one!'

'They're all brothers and sisters though,' the lady with the clipboard pointed out, reasonably.

'Please don't split us up!' said an older boy, desperately, suddenly, and May's heart went out to him as she saw his pale and anxious face, the way he put his arm around his little sister and gave her a fierce hug, despite the fact that she had clearly wet her knickers on the long journey from London.

'I said, just one!' snapped the lady, and when the other woman nodded wearily, she snatched up a trunk, grabbed the hand of the little girl, and made to drag her away from her brother's encircling arms. The whole platform turned and stared as she screamed in terror, her brother bursting out into helpless tears at the same time, trying in vain to clutch at her flailing hand.

May turned away from the sight, sickened and frightened by what she had witnessed. She had hoped this would be better here, that those untouched by the bombing would find some compassion for those fleeing the Blitz. At least, that's what they'd told her at the office when she'd gone to sign up for evacuation, she reflected, bitterly.

When her turn came, she steeled herself for the worst. A stern-faced lady approached the woman with the clipboard and frowned when she saw May.

'I said, no children,' she barked, abruptly. The woman smiled weakly and tried to joke, 'Well it isn't born yet.' Unamused, the lady turned to May and said, 'When are you due?'

May drew a deep, steadying breath.

'Next month, sometime,' she said calmly, 'I shan't be any trouble.'

The lady nodded curtly, looked back at the woman.

'I'm assuming there is no choice?' she asked, rudely, and the woman shook her head mutely and put a tiny tick on the bottom of her clipboard.

And suddenly May was following her, trudging along the street lugging her trunk behind her. No offer of help was given, none taken. May bit her lip angrily, refused to give in and ask for what the lady clearly begrudged her. The baby kicked against the strain, and May had to stop for a moment, bracing herself with an involuntary gasp against the internal onslaught. The lady turned and scowled threateningly.

'You'd better not have it there,' she hissed, nastily. 'We're here now anyway,' and she turned and ran up the steps of the big house with the black railings May was using to support herself.

May tilted her chin defiantly, refusing to give in to how she was feeling in front of this awful, hateful woman. Furiously, she snatched up her trunk and heaved it up the steps, ignoring the inner commotion this action drew forth. She followed her silently into what was clearly an unused front room, two sofas perched primly around an empty, cold grate.

'My name is Mrs Harding,' the woman snapped. 'You can make up a bed behind the sofa each night, I've put you a sleeping roll and blankets out. You can eat in the kitchen when Mr Harding and myself have breakfasted. And I'll thank you to leave the house by eight every morning, and not to return before eight each evening!'

May stared at her, aghast. Whatever would she do for twelve hours a day in a strange town, dragging her protesting bump around with her? Taking a deep breath, she mustered her pride and forced herself to smile brightly, determined not to let her see that she had got to her. Determined to show better manners than this hard-faced, stuck-up woman.

'Thank you so much for having me,' she answered politely, then stiffly turned her back on her to begin making up her meagre bed, ignoring the clawing of hunger from her guts as she was damned if she was going to ask for her tea now, despite having been on the train for the best part of the day.

She lay awake most of that long, troubled night, the thin bedroll doing little to cushion her from the unforgiving boards beneath her aching back. When the baby's kicks became too insistent to lie there for a moment longer, she finally capitulated and rolled up her bedding, stood staring out of the bay window into the street below, screwing her gritty eyes up against the grim light of dawn.

When she finally heard the front door bang, she watched for a moment as the unknown Mr Harding left the house for work, his shoulders hunched against the early morning chill. Or was it just against his miserable wife, wondered May naughtily, a touch of her old mischievous grin twitching up the corners of her mouth, making her realise just how long it had been since she'd last smiled.

Breakfast was an unprepossessing affair, some dry toast and a glass of milk seemed to be all that there was on offer. Mrs Harding walked in as May was washing up her plate and stood staring at her silently from the doorway, then made her jump by clearing her throat noisily.

'You're pregnant,' she stated, rather unnecessarily, May thought, struggling to stifle the giggle that rose up unbidden and unwanted, desperately trying not to think about what Janie might have said next. 'You must have a special rations book then, for extra?' May nodded reluctantly, wondering where this was going.

'Well hand it over then,' said Mrs Harding briskly, 'I'll be needing that to feed you, and no doubt you'll be hungrier than most with that lump on you!'

May paused, trying not to lash out with the sharp edge of her tongue. Much as she hated this woman, she needed the bed, dared not go back to London with the bombs falling nightly when she had no idea when she might need to go into hospital. At the same time, she was determined not to let Mrs Harding win this little battle, the first of many in their own, private little war.

'I understood you wanted me out from under your feet from eight 'til eight,' she offered, demurely, 'and as you're right, I get hungry with the baby coming, I need to eat earlier than that, and

I'd hate to disturb you and your husband's evening meal anyway. I'll just keep myself to myself and collect my own rations, I'll fix my own food to make myself less of a burden to you.'

She smiled sweetly at Mrs Harding from under her long lashes, triumphantly enjoying the look of consternation swiftly masked on the older woman's greedy face.

And that evening, footsore and exhausted, she sat and licked the fresh butter off her fingers, knowing that Mrs Harding was watching her furiously and furtively from across the kitchen, and enjoyed the rich taste all the more.

The day that May left, Lydia spent hours on her feet in the shop, stock-taking and serving customers, and longing with all her heart for Millie to drop in after her shift to lend a hand as she so often did these days. Running the place single-handed was tough, but actually Lydia had taken to it gladly when Stanley left, glad to be out of the house, the big house which felt so, so empty now. And today she desperately needed the distraction from the memory of her sister's white-faced misery as they'd hugged good-bye at the station, and she yearned for Millie's cheeriness so much more than she needed her practical help.

She straightened up from stacking the lower shelves and clutched at the counter as she felt the world shift on its axis. She smiled wryly as gradually her dizziness passed, she had no real idea yet how far gone she was, but she knew for sure that she was pregnant.

She had not told a soul, not even Arthur, who was spending most of his off-duty time with her now, the two of them cocooned in their own little world. She hugged the secret to her for now, enjoying the private knowledge of the new little life, unafraid, uncaring of what people would say, just happy to know she carried his baby within. She knew she should act soon and tell him of her condition, that she should be ashamed of being pregnant out of wedlock, but, Lydia reasoned sadly, with half the world hell-bent on fighting the other half, what would they care anyway?

With a clatter of heels on the wooden step, Millie arrived then looked at her sharply, instantly taking note of Lydia's wan demeanour.

'You're missing her already, aren't you?' she clucked sympathetically. 'Go and put a pot of tea on out the back and I'll finish up here.'

Lydia nodded mutely, suddenly feeling so tearful she did not trust herself to speak. She turned abruptly and went to boil the kettle on the little gas stove they kept for long days at work, thankful for a moment of peace to rest her feet and stretch her aching back.

By the time Millie had joined her she had recovered herself, was ready to hold her head high and show that all was well. Millie smiled at her and took the proffered tea-cup from her hands, took a long gulp of the strong brew and sat down in companionable silence. Both women were working longer and longer hours, and even now, they were not finished. Every night that they could, they would spend out in the garden, tending the vegetables that now dominated the beds previously bright with flowers. 'Growing for England' was on everybody's lips, and they were both determined to do their bit.

Eventually, Lydia put down her empty cup with a grimace, then smiled grimly at Millie.

'Better get a move on then,' she said firmly, and with that, they both stood and walked determinedly out of the door and back up the hill to the next task in hand.

The days blurred into a haze of fatigue and loneliness. May left early each morning, walked up and down the high street of the pretty little market town until she could no longer carry the weight of her ever-expanding bump. Eventually, she would go to the public baths, paying sixpence for the privilege from her carefully hoarded earnings to luxuriate in a tub of warm water in a tiny cubicle, separated from the next woman and the next by thinly partitioned walls. Then, and only then, as weightlessness relieved her heavy body, would she let her thoughts wander, giving in to the loneliness and weeping softly, her salty tears mingling with the water. Missing Lydia, missing Millie and Janie, missing the camaraderie of the big house. Not, she realised, in a rare moment of bleak honesty, not missing Jimmy.

Then, when her time was up, she would pull herself together and towel herself down briskly to return to the high street, whiling her time away in the little library and queueing, always queueing, for food. She took great pleasure in finding a quiet bench in the park to eat her lunch, forcing herself not to give into the noisy begging from the sparrows that would materialise to share her bench with her, cheering her up with their chatter that reminded her so much of home. She took even greater pleasure in eating her tea in front of the Hardings, saving the best bits until the evening so that they could see what she was allowed and what they were missing.

And then one day, it happened. She had just got out of the bath when she felt a warm rush of fluid as her waters broke, and grabbing the door handle for support, May tried not to panic as the first wave of pain threatened to engulf her, making her struggle for breath.

'Are you all right in there?' asked a concerned voice suddenly, coming from somewhere nearby.

'No. Yes. I mean, no, no, no!' gasped May, suddenly elated but afraid, so, so afraid. 'I think my baby is coming.'

'Open the door, love,' said the voice calmly, but May shook her head frantically, then laughed hysterically as she realised the owner of the voice couldn't see her.

'I'm not dressed,' she managed, then began to laugh and cry at the same time, the strain of the past few weeks erupting from her in waves.

Then looked up in shock as a face appeared over the partition, followed by a leg, then a person, a young woman, about Lydia's age, dropping over the cubicle wall.

'As it happens, you're in luck,' she murmured soothingly as she reached for May's clothes, pulling her dress over her unprotesting head, 'I'm a nurse. You need go to hospital now, love.'

May would wish later that she could remember the woman's name, wasn't even sure she had asked it. By the time she had been led, hand in hand up the high street to the little cottage hospital, the pains were coming thick and fast, and she could no longer speak. She endured an examination by an exhausted looking midwife, who pronounced that she was 'in for a long run', then left her alone in the white, cold labour ward, struggling not to give way to the screams that threatened to escape her.

And as she lay and laboured to bring their child into the world, Jimmy lay silently in his dugout a world away, breathing noiselessly, awaiting the order to fall back. Waiting to begin the job he was trained to do, disabling any machinery or vehicles they were forced to leave behind so they could not fall into the hands of the advancing enemy. Fighting back his fear of being left behind, of being captured.

Equally unlooked for and unguessed at, Lydia crouched trembling, panting with fright in the privy of the big house, desperately trying to mop up the flow of dark blood running down her thighs. Beginning, with harsh, lonely sobs, to mourn the child she would never have.

And just when May thought she could bear it no more on that long, dark day, that her body and soul would surely be torn apart by the ravages of the pain, she remembered finally how to protect herself, and began to slowly, deliberately retreat from the agony of her current existence into a different place far beyond where the pain could reach her.

When the midwife looked in on her later, she drew her breath in shock, thinking that she must have haemorrhaged, must have surely died. May was still and silent, and lay sublimely unaware as she assessed her, but the midwife's practised eye saw that her tiny frame was still wracked by the force of the contractions. Realising that May was no longer able to give any more effort and that she was utterly spent, the midwife leant over swiftly and pressed with all her weight on May's midriff as she saw the next contraction sweep over her body, the body which, despite the withdrawal of her conscious mind, was determined to struggle onwards and give birth. The baby was born with the minimum of fuss moments later, and only then, as the squalling infant was lifted onto her breast did May stir from her private, safe place, looking down at the baby with such tenderness and love that the midwife had to look away and brush tears from her eyes.

'You had a bad time there,' she said brusquely, then caught the bemused look on May's exhausted but now radiant face.

'Not me, no,' she answered, genuinely puzzled, 'not me. Maybe it was someone else you heard?'

And she turned away, lost in the moment, nuzzling her baby like every new mother animal before her, drinking in the scent

and feel of her new baby, oblivious to all around her as she sa-
voured those most precious and most intimate of moments with
the tiny being that was her daughter.

Nobody came to visit. May spent the next three days recovering from what she finally came to understand had been a
long and traumatic ordeal, and it seemed her torn and bleeding
body was not ready to be sent home just yet. She would come to
remember those days later as a tiny, warm hiatus of time, explor-
ing her baby daughter's little body and learning to survive the first
demands and hurdles of motherhood.

When her baby cried, she refused the kindly and well-meant
offer from a nurse to take her away to the large nursery down the
corridor so that May could sleep. Instead, she rocked and sang and
walked back and forth to soothe her, relishing the moment when
the tiny girl would succumb to sleep and go limp and heavy in her
arms, when she could gaze at her perfect little black lashes and
almond-shaped eyes as she slept.

She named her Irene. It was a family tradition to name babies
after previous family members, but the rebellious streak in May
reared its head suddenly; she would call her daughter by a name
of her own choice, her very own, with no need to ask Jimmy or
anyone else, for that matter.

'She's mine,' thought May fiercely, as she watched her baby
sleep, 'and it's no one's business but mine.'

On the fourth day, a nurse came to check little Irene, and to
May's astonishment and delight, it was the same nurse who had
vaulted over the partition wall at the baths to help her when she
first went into labour. She looked May straight in the eye and
grinned sympathetically.

'You had a bad time there,' she observed. She looked at May's wan face, and grimaced, 'but I'm afraid we don't have room for you now. We need to discharge you today. I'm so sorry.'

May nodded, swallowing hard. She had been expecting this, she had spent most of yesterday up and about and knew they would not be able to keep her for much longer. She looked up to find the nurse watching her closely.

'Is everything all right?' she ventured quietly.

May looked down at her hands doing her utmost to quell the despair rising within.

'Everything's fine,' she replied, firmly, then burst out, 'I just wish I could go home! I hate it here!' And with that, she burst out into choking sobs, causing Irene to stir, then fret.

The nurse sighed and took her hand.

'Is it that bad?' she asked, gently, and when May wept harder, she said, 'Is there nowhere else you could go?'

May shook her head, grimly, desperately trying to regain her composure whilst jiggling the now howling Irene on her shoulder.

'I'll just have to put up with it,' she muttered. 'It's not that bad. I don't mind.'

But when May winced her painful way up the steps of the forbidding house, her courage almost failed her. Mrs Harding stood looking down at her, her arms folded across her chest, making no move to help May who was struggling with her bag and little Irene, a cold hard look in her eyes.

'I said, no children,' she snapped, icily, not once looking at the tiny baby asleep in May's arms, glaring at May as if she had dirtied her precious house, 'I don't have to have you here, you know!'

May went to answer, made to apologise, then stopped herself

as Irene snuggled more closely against her. She would not apologise for this child, she would not try to ingratiate herself with this hateful woman.

For the first time in her young life, May did not back down.

'Excuse me,' she said quietly and politely, calmly stepping past Mrs Harding and walking into the front room that had represented her home for the past month. As she had suspected, her sleeping roll was gone, and her meagre possessions were stuffed in the trunk she had arrived with on that inauspicious day. The place felt as cold and unwelcoming as the owner, and in that moment, May's mind was made up.

She turned on her heel and faced Mrs Harding, who took an involuntary step back when faced with the barely controlled fury on May's face.

'Please call us a cab,' she said, tightly, and when Mrs Harding asked her to where, she glared at her again and said, 'Why, to the station of course. I'd rather spend the night in the air-raid shelter than another under your roof.'

And with that, she swept out of the door to await her cab; London, her sisters and the Blitz suddenly infinitely preferable to one more moment enduring the stony dislike of the most appropriately named Mrs Harding.

When Arthur came to see Lydia on that terrible day, he knocked at the back door for some time, puzzled that she didn't seem to be in. He ceased knocking for a moment and squinted through the kitchen window, straining to focus through the lace curtains that Lydia struggled to replace every morning after removing the blackouts, a task she had stubbornly insisted upon since the beginning of the war.

He was about to turn on his heel and leave when he thought he heard a tiny sound, a little gasp, almost a sob. He stopped in his tracks, whirled around to try to identify the source of the sound, then ran towards the privy door.

'Lydia?' he asked tentatively, then stopped, appalled as the door swung slowly open, revealing the desperate plight of the broken woman inside.

Arthur swallowed hard and bit back his cry of horror as he saw his Lydia, his woman, collapsed on the bare, unforgiving floor, blood soaking the lower half of her body. She looked up at him piteously, and in a moment he understood what he was seeing and swept her up into his arms, trying not to show his instinctive revulsion as her bloodied hands reached up to cling around his neck. Holding her as gently as he could manage, he shouldered the kitchen door open roughly and stepped into the bizarre normality of the kitchen, betrayed only by three tiny splashes of blood spattered and drying on the normally pristine floor-boards.

Pausing to catch his breath, he climbed steadily up the stairs to the little back room over the kitchen, the room he had grown to love as he had consummated his love for the woman now lying barely conscious in his arms. Trying hard to contain his own emotion, his own guilt, he laid her gently on the bed and brushed her hair back out of her eyes. Seeing that she was shivering, he pulled the blanket out from underneath her and tucked her up, shocked by the sudden keening sound this drew from her bloodless lips.

'Lydia?' he asked, desperately, needing to connect with her, frantic to draw her back from the dark place she had withdrawn to.

She keened again, a weak, sobbing noise, her hands clutching the blanket and curling her legs up against her chest. Frightened now, Arthur went to the window, and to his enormous relief, saw

Millie walking up the hill, she had clearly finished her shift and was on her way home.

'Stay there, Lydia,' he said, pointlessly, 'I'll be straight back,' and ran down the stairs two at a time, almost knocking Millie over in his haste as she walked into the kitchen.

'I've just been to the shop and it's closed, Lydia's not there,' she began, then looked at Arthur aghast as he collapsed into a chair, tears welling up in his eyes.

'She's here,' he said, then gathered himself with a visible effort to look Millie straight in the eye, 'and she's just lost our baby.'

After the doctor left, Millie and Arthur sat quietly in the kitchen, both nursing a cup of much-needed, strong tea. Lydia was still upstairs, mercifully cleaned up and asleep now with the heavy sedation the doctor had given her. Arthur looked at Millie, went to say something, then stopped, unable to find the right words.

'It's all right,' she said gently, 'I do understand you know. In fact, I'm glad, glad that you two at least have each other!' She stopped too, the emotion and the trauma finally hitting her, suddenly missing Stanley desperately on this dreadful, bleak day. Seeing her distress, Arthur jumped up and went to give her an awkward hug, both of them aware of the mutual craving for simple physical comfort.

'I just hope she feels better tomorrow,' he said quietly, 'I just need to talk to her. I didn't know about the baby, Millie, I didn't know!' And with that, the tears came again, and both of them sat in the evening light, both consumed by their own misery, neither able to be brave on this dark night.

And when the air-raid warning came, neither heeded the sound, Millie choosing to remain alone in the kitchen with her tea,

Arthur retreating upstairs to lie next to Lydia, his arms wrapped around her unresponsive body, hoping against hope that she would glean some small comfort from this simple connection, this little but heartfelt act of love.

When May walked in through the door holding little Irene against her breast like a talisman, she stood stock still, abruptly aware that something fundamental had changed.

For a moment, she could not place it. Then gradually, it came to her, seeping like damp, then a cold flood of realisation.

The kitchen was empty. The kitchen was dirty. Not very dirty, just not pristine, the way her mother, the way Lydia would have left it. When she squinted critically at the floor, she could see three distinct areas that looked different, as if they had been scrubbed and scoured recently, but the rest looked dull and unloved, as if the cleaner had simply wiped around a cursory mop, uncaring of and not looking for satisfaction in the result.

May looked about her, confused, fear gripping her deep inside. Lydia should be here now, it was after shop closing time and she had just walked past it on her way up the hill and seen the closed sign in the window. Maybe she was out tending her vegetables? May scooped Irene higher on her shoulder and went to the stairs, realising she needed to settle Irene and take stock of the situation.

As she walked into her bedroom, she caught her breath as she saw the bed, felt the visceral memory of Jimmy assailing her with its ferocity and power. She shut her eyes momentarily and steadied herself against the door frame, then jumped again as she heard a noise her, a noise coming from Lydia's room. The sound of desperate, despairing sobbing. The sound of a woman incoherent with grief. Unmistakably Lydia, unmistakably her sister.

Breathing hard and suddenly terrified by what she might find, May settled Irene down in her little carry cot, well away from the bed which had stirred such a wealth of painful memories. Swiftly, she walked across the landing and pushed open the door and went in quickly, went to the untidy bed from where the sound was emanating. As she put her hand tentatively onto the mound of blankets, the weeping stopped abruptly, and Lydia raised her swollen face to May, her tangled hair falling in clumps over her eyes.

Both sisters stared at one another, both equally shocked. May wordlessly taking in her sister's dishevelled appearance, Lydia disorientated, confused by May's very presence, May, who should be in Hertfordshire, safe from the incessant, exhausting air-raids. Then both began to laugh and cry at the same time, May clinging to her older sister with all the emotion that the loneliness and fear of the past few weeks had instilled within her, the need for her family at the most important time of her life surfacing like an open wound, Lydia with the raw pain of an unshared horror, the need to share and find compassion and understanding suddenly uncontrollable.

Both talked at the same time, then stopped and wept again. Then May held Lydia for a long time, as painfully she began to talk, slowly at first, then faster and faster as if she could expunge the pain just by forcing the story out, word by jagged word, to someone who would listen. May listened silently, tears rolling down her face as Lydia told her of her tiny dead baby, the fear and the blood. Her fear that she would die alone, then hoping that she would indeed die, before anyone could find her, make her live to see and cope with what she had lost. The dashing of a dream.

'When did it happen, lovey?' she asked, tenderly, still reeling at the sight of her sister's despair. Lydia lay back on the rumpled pillow and thought, rubbing her swollen eyes tiredly with the backs of her hands.

'I don't really know,' she answered, in a bemused voice, 'it must have been a while though. Arthur's been looking after me, and Millie's been looking after the shop so I haven't been out since.'

May gazed at her, shocked by the defeat in her eyes. Before the enormity of her sister's pain, she faltered at first when she told her own story, feeling her own inadequacy before Lydia's desolation. But gradually Lydia began to listen, began to respond to May, shaking her head vehemently against the cruelty May had borne, agreeing fervently with her decision to come home to London and her family. Then almost as if she had recovered, she sat up, straightened her crumpled dress and suggested that they go and prepare food together, ready for when Millie and Arthur would arrive home.

May looked at Lydia questioningly when she mentioned Arthur, and suddenly a snapshot of the old Lydia surfaced, stuck a stubborn chin up in the air with a flash of her usual defiance that May knew and loved so well.

'Yes, Arthur is staying here,' she said firmly, 'there's a war on and the whole world is doing what they like, and nobody's bloody well going to stop us!'

But as they walked slowly down the stairs together, May swallowed back more tears as she realised sadly that not once had Lydia asked to see the baby. Not once.

Much later that night, May was sitting quietly by the stove nursing Irene while Lydia and Millie slept upstairs. The clock ticked steadily and she began to doze, Irene's milky warmth against her heart soothing her from the torment that her sister had described to her during this strange and exhausting day.

All of a sudden, the kitchen door clicked and swung open. For a moment, May was rooted to the spot with shock, then breathed out a hiss of relief as Arthur shut the door and flicked on the light, jumping as much as she had when he laid eyes on her.

'May!' he cried out, startled, then greedily, 'Can I see the baby?'

Reaching out gently, he took the swaddled little bundle from her arms, and sat drinking in the sight of Irene's contented little face, half asleep but lips still working determinedly as if she was yet to realise that she was no longer feeding. May looked at him carefully before she said anything, then saw the tears in his eyes and reached out to touch his shoulder.

'When did it happen?' she asked quietly, and when Arthur raised his stricken face to hers, she saw the pain etched deep on his features.

'It was the same day as you had your Irene,' he answered painfully. 'And May, she hasn't been up since. She just cries and cries and there's nothing I can do to help her. She barely eats, and she isn't sleeping, I just don't know what to do.'

May gazed at him, shocked to the core by what she was hearing. Lydia was the strong one, the one who coped, the one they all leaned on. It was Lydia who picked up the pieces when Mum died, and then again when they lost Dad. Lydia just could not fall apart, what would happen to the rest of them if she did? The selfishness of that thought suddenly rocked her and almost took her breath away. It was her turn to help Lydia now, it was her sister who now needed the support, and May was determined to give it, no matter how strangely the role sat on her shoulders.

'She was up today,' May said, 'and I'll make sure she gets up and gets washed tomorrow. Then I'll see if I can get her out into the fresh air. Little steps, Arthur. We have to start somewhere.'

And with that, she kissed his forehead and took Irene from his arms, noting the involuntary twist of pain on his face as she did so.

'Go to bed, Arthur,' she said softly. 'I need to get an early start to sort the house out, and then I'm going to make a start with Lydia. It's going to be all right.'

Time slipped by. Weeks became months, a bizarre normality creeping in to going to bed in an air-raid shelter, adults sleeping barely a breath away from one another, babies cradled close. Emerging blinking into the dusty brightness of the morning, tired minds dimly registering damage done, houses fallen, houses still standing.

Night after night.

Millie and Arthur became the lynchpins of that damaged little household in the big, empty house. The newcomers recognised what was needed, how to support the sisters while time passed, hoping that if they could give them enough time they could both come to terms with their new lives, accept what had happened to them both.

And in so many ways, it seemed that normality had indeed returned. Lydia emerged slowly from her cocoon, coaxed, encouraged and bullied by May to rejoin the ranks of the walking wounded. It almost seemed that she had moved on from her tragic loss, had forgotten the day she lay in her own blood and wished to die. And it seemed that May had adjusted to becoming a mother, and that tucking a baby up while bombs fell around them was an acceptable life. That choosing between a Mickey Mouse and a Donald Duck gas mask for her toddling daughter on her first morning at playgroup was somehow exciting and fun.

The fact that Lydia was civil to Irene and often chatted to her over breakfast, but never, ever held her, kissed her, or swept her up in her arms for a cuddle was never discussed.

Millie and Arthur held them all together in those strange months and years, formed the heart of Irene's family, loved her unconditionally, the two of them not only supporting May as she brought Irene up, but filling in the yawning void left by her lack of a father figure, and the unexplained absence of an aunt's love and affection, despite the tangible presence of her mother's sister. A presence that seemed to wax and wane with the tides, sometimes cheerful, bossy and seemingly indestructible; sometimes brittle, weepy and withdrawn. An aunt who held the household together with her cooking and singing, then a shadow of an aunt who would disappear to bed, neither stirring nor eating for days at a time.

The little girl did as so many did in those war years, she grew and flourished in her extended family, never knowing what she was missing, simply accepting life as it came to her. Learning to run to the shelter without waiting or looking back if she heard an incoming doodlebug, slinging her gas mask over her shoulder as she went off to playgroup. Her own little tragedies, an unkind friend, a lost teddy, more relevant and distressing in her toddler world than the ruins of the neighbouring house, than the woman sobbing uncontrollably on her doorstep with a telegram in her hand.

Time went by, and life went on.

And then one night, Jimmy came home.

Part Five

Spring 1944, Father and Daughter

The boys of the Eighth Army were due a rest. Jimmy came home from Africa, from the desert, exhausted, dusty and dark-skinned, lifting his tired face to the soft rain in the cool London morning with something close to rapture. He paused for a long moment on the platform of the station, then saw Arthur striding towards him, like a vision of someone he had known a lifetime ago.

The two men looked at each other, paused infinitesimally, a tiny, awkward moment, then Arthur reached out his hand to cross the unacknowledged divide and shook Jimmy's, smiling a guarded welcome.

'How's May?' asked Jimmy, gruffly and was rewarded by a wide grin from the other man.

'She's a natural mother,' he answered with pride in his voice, 'you just wait and see, she's wonderful with her.'

Jimmy looked sideways then, was it a shifty look or was he just anxious to get to Muswell Hill, Arthur wondered, suspiciously. Lydia had confided her fears about Jimmy long ago, and although Arthur had not seen any evidence for himself, he was wary of this intense, brooding young man.

Jimmy took his leave of Arthur then, walked purposefully out of the station and up the hill. When he reached the big house, he realised his palms were sweating and that his heart was beating painfully in his chest. After four long years, meeting his own child felt strangely intimidating, and he smiled grimly to himself when he thought of the conditions under which he had been fighting, the dust and the heat, the ever present fear of capture, of injury, of death. He took a long, steadying breath and walked through the kitchen door.

His eyes fell on the tiny figure of a woman at the sink, her back to him but already turning, startled by his unexpected entrance. For a fleeting moment he saw May, then his mind adjusted and he saw Lydia, older, equally beautiful, but lacking May's vibrancy, somehow ethereal, insubstantial.

She looked exhausted, he realised. The daily grind of the war, the relentless air raids, the rationing, the extra workload, were all taking their toll. Jimmy had no idea what those at home were coping with, but he could read the strain on Lydia's tired features.

She pushed her hair back from her eyes and offered a smile. Then suddenly she shrugged and reached out spontaneously to hug her brother-in-law, the need for human contact driving them both past former mistrust and doubt. When he pulled away and looked at her questioningly, she shook her head helplessly and gestured to the door.

'She went to check the veggies,' she offered lamely. 'Up the hill, the old green on the left. Irene's with her.'

'Irene?' He tried the name on his lips, rolling his tongue around his unknown daughter's unfamiliar name.

'You didn't know?' asked Lydia, her shock showing on her thin face as she looked at him, puzzled.

'The letters never reach us,' answered Jimmy, bitterly, 'I never even knew what we'd had. I never knew her name.'

They locked gazes for a long moment, Lydia wondering suddenly if May had ever written at all. For she and Millie had written to Stanley, to Reggie and Bert, and although their replies came back with heavy censor lines struck cruelly through the details for which they so desperately craved, they had managed to glean more information than it seemed Jimmy was privy to.

He took a deep breath then and smiled at her bleakly.

'Irene,' he said again, musingly, turned on his heel and strode out of the door.

At the top of the hill was an old Victorian garden, black iron railings around it, the gates open for the first time in his memory. He walked through quietly, the watery light of the early spring day seeping through the trees and alighting upon a vision he could not quite believe, a vision so far removed from the dry heat of the desert that he stumbled slightly, unable to comprehend what his senses were telling him.

A woman, dark curls falling over her face, her little waist cinched in with an apron clearly made from the remains of another dress, familiar somehow, but not that he could place at that moment. A little figure next to her, a tiny but exquisite replica, pulling at a weed with all her might, giggling with pleasure as the root suddenly gave way making her stagger back into the ever ready arms of her doting mother.

Then suddenly the vision stiffened and clutched the child to her, wiping her hands nervously on her apron. Shielding her eyes from the low rays of the sun, she squinted towards him, uncertainly.

'Jimmy?' she breathed, unbelieving. Then, consumed by all the love she had ever felt for this man, swept along by the seductive tide of her lost dreams, May let go of the child's hand, and ran into his arms as if she were nineteen again, giving her lips up, her body up to the passion of the moment.

It took a while before either of them became aware of it, an eternity before they turned to hear the tiny sound of distress emanating from the little girl standing desolate beside them.

Alone. Abandoned.

For the first time in her life.

Jimmy had two weeks. A mere two weeks to recover from the desert, to reacquaint himself with his wife and to become a father to his mistrustful little girl.

For the first few days, Irene was reticent and drew back when he approached. Frankly, Jimmy barely noticed, he was so swept up by London life again, persuading May to come out west with him in the early evening, dancing like the old days in the little halls they used to frequent, kissing and drinking and laughing once again, the only difference being the blackout curtains blocking out the streets outside, streets no longer full of bustle and life, but deserted as soon as dusk fell.

Then finally, Jimmy did begin to notice his beautiful daughter, became enthralled by the way her tight black ringlets bounced when she threw back her head and laughed, her infectious giggles bringing a smile to the faces of all those around her.

Each morning, she would chatter over breakfast, Arthur smiling benignly at her, May, Lydia and Millie laughing along with the cheery little girl, unperturbed by spending the night cheek by jowl with her mother in the air raid shelter, each and every night now. But one morning, she became aware of her father watching her, became self-conscious, fell silent.

'Tell me about school, my angel,' he encouraged her, but Irene stayed silent, not liking being called 'angel' by a man she barely knew. Jimmy persisted and went a step further: 'Come and sit on my lap and tell me about school.'

Irene cleared her throat nervously and glanced around her at the encouraging faces of the people in her little world that she knew and trusted. Hesitantly, she clambered up on to Jimmy's lap and cleared her throat again, looking desperately at her mother for support and inspiration. She opened her mouth, but although she truly meant to try, nothing came forth, besides the sound of her urgently clearing her throat again, beset by nerves.

'Stop clearing your throat and talk to me!' said Jimmy, awkwardly, aware of everyone looking on, knowing that he was a stranger in their midst.

He looked down at Irene then, hiding from their gazes, and his eyes fell upon the tiny miniature of his wife looking mutely up at him, both looking for a connection, to broach the void between them. Without stopping to think, he bent and kissed her cheek tenderly, unwittingly grazing her slightly with his stubble. And in the space of a heartbeat, their connection ended. Irene reared backwards and screamed in shock, clutching her hands to her face and scrambling towards the nearest familiar figure, her beloved Aunt Millie, who swept her up with understanding arms.

Jimmy leapt to his feet, humiliated, embarrassed and anxious to cover it, his chair falling over with a crash behind him, unnoticed.

'Tonight, you'll learn to answer me when I speak to you!' he shouted furiously, his temper seething dangerously, publically, close to the surface. 'And your mother had better make sure you know how to address your elders and betters!'

Then he turned and stormed up the stairs, the sound of the slamming bedroom door reverberating over the muffled, piteous sound of his daughter's terrified sobs.

U nder the watchful eye of Arthur, the pieces were picked up carefully, without anyone acknowledging what had just happened. May got Irene ready for school, then left to work on the communal vegetable patch, scuttling hurriedly out of the door without a word, without a backwards glance. Shocked by what she had just witnessed, Millie walked Irene up to school on her way to work, the little girl clutching her hand tightly with one hand, her other holding her Donald Duck gas mask firmly to her chest. With a sigh, Lydia stood and silently began to clear away the breakfast things, mentally calculating what she could use to put dinner together for six hungry people on today's remaining rations.

She jumped when Arthur went to hold her, reaching his long arms around and nuzzling his face in to the back of her neck as she bent over the sink.

'Oh Arthur,' she sighed, leaning back against him, savouring the moment with just the two of them, perfectly attuned. He spun her around, hugged her hard.

'What on earth was that all about?' she asked, softly. Arthur shook his head. 'He just seemed to explode for no reason, he frightened poor little Irene so much she just couldn't talk!' she burst out, her own anger and indignation now surfacing.

They stayed there for a while, finding solace in each other's company, in each other's concern. They knew they needed to ward off Jimmy's temper to protect Irene, but at the same time, they were both acutely aware that it should really be up to May to do this, and also that Jimmy would be counting the days left to him now and must be desperate to connect with his daughter and enjoy the simple pleasures of a child's unconditional, trusting love before returning to the bitter reality of the war. They could hardly stand in his way as he tried to talk to her, in fact the more they thought about it, the harder it was to understand why the situation had escalated so rapidly.

Had it, perhaps, been Irene's fault after all?

The evening passed peacefully, and for once, there was no air raid. May seemed at her best, impeccably dressed, despite the shortages, her dress emphasizing her tiny waist and showing her shapely legs. In fact, when Lydia looked more closely, she realised that she must have asked Millie to paint a line down the backs of her calves in gravy powder, the measure they had all taken to in the past year to look like they were wearing seamed stockings, the real things now like gold dust and too costly on the black market.

May sparkled that night. She fluttered like a beautiful butterfly between Jimmy and Irene, one moment jiggling her daughter on her knee, singing nursery rhymes, the next laughing and flirting with her husband.

The morning's tension appeared to have dissipated, and everybody began to relax and enjoy the relative freedom of spending the evening in the house without having to go to the claustrophobic little shelter. Irene also seemed happy, revelling in the attention from her mother, her uncle and her aunts and daring to show off a little for the benefit of the unknown father she so wanted

117

to impress, who was now smiling benignly at her across the big scrubbed table.

Lydia and Arthur left to go upstairs first, neither of them needing to say a word, both perfectly aware of one another's feelings since their quiet little wedding, a world away from what the teenage Lydia had once dreamed of, but so much happier than she could have imagined, so full of calm understanding. They smiled their goodnights from the bottom of the stairs, Arthur sweeping Irene up into his arms for a quick cuddle. He noted sadly that Lydia turned away then, she still had never kissed nor held Irene, never once shared her bedtime rituals of cuddles. After those first bleak days after losing their baby, she had seemed to put it behind her, although every so often it seemed the demons would arise to reclaim her, sending her weeping to her bed for what seemed like an eternity each time. Then she would recover, rising valiantly to reclaim her place in the heart of the house and the family, but never had she been able to find joy in the simple affection radiating from the happy little girl in their midst.

Millie stood and went to the sink to rinse her glass, gave May and Irene a kiss and waved to Jimmy as she went to the stairs, her loneliness suddenly palpable in the room. When she reached her bedroom, she stood stock still for a moment inside the doorway, trying desperately to feel some essence of Stanley, some sign that her short marriage was real, had ever even existed. Her eyes fell on the desk and she went over to it sadly, opening the folder he had left there when he was last home.

He had not been home since Dunkirk. She shuddered as her eyes fell on that stark drawing, remembering Stanley's halting voice as he had recounted the terrible story of the rout from the beach, the searing sadness of meeting but not being able to save Edward, that brave young man who had fought twice for his country and died on that bleak seashore, like so many who would never be buried in the land of their birth.

She turned the page, full of sorrow, then with the next picture, came the tears. She wept at the sight of a laughing young girl, innocent of the horrors that their generation would need to face up to, so happy and hopeful for her future, for their future. So full of love and promise.

Eventually, she climbed stiffly into her cold bed, and hugging Stanley's bolster against her body she let the hot tears fall until finally sleep released her from her anguish of missing her young husband, of not knowing and not being able to help him with whatever burden he must surely now be struggling to bear.

May looked at her young husband and daughter, alone for the first time as a family since Jimmy had returned almost a week ago. She felt full of hope and love, the flare of anger this morning now dismissed in her mind as a temporary irritability, after all, Irene's nervous habit of clearing her throat constantly could be annoying, and surely she could have been a little more acquiescent, gone to her father with open arms as she did to the rest of the family? Except Lydia, she thought, grimly, then, as May always did with unpleasant thoughts, she simply put this reality out of her mind and replaced it with a beaming smile.

Jimmy returned her smile and held his hand out, whistling a little refrain, and catching her hand he spun her round in a quick twirl. May laughed out loud, leant back into Jimmy's arms and twirled again, Irene looking on delightedly from the other side of the table. Tentatively, Jimmy reached out his other hand to her, and suddenly all three of them were spinning around the furniture, stamping their feet and clicking their fingers to an imaginary rhythm they could all hear, united by the thrill of the dance.

Finally they all stopped, hot and happy and laughing. May looked at Jimmy as he led the way upstairs with Irene's little hand clutched firmly in his, and felt her heart overflow with love as her eyes did suddenly with joyful tears.

As they undressed to go to bed, Irene tucked up snugly in the little bunk they had made for her in the bay window, Jimmy paused and looked at May for a long moment.

'I want our own place,' he said abruptly. 'I want it to be just us, just the three of us, in a place we can call our own.'

May looked at him, caught unawares, the thought of being alone for the unknown duration of the war scaring her.

'I know, love,' she offered gently, 'but it is nice being here with Lydia and Millie while you boys are away, and Arthur is such a darling, it's good for Irene to have a father figure around…'

She petered out, uncertainly, seeing a dark shadow descend across Jimmy's face.

'I just meant it's nice to have a man around the house to look after us all,' she whispered, frightened now, then in the next instant, knew she had made a mistake.

'So you like a man about the house, do you?' snarled Jimmy, feeling the rage bubble unchecked in his chest. 'Not much of a man, though, to be skulking at home with all the girls while we're all out fighting, is he!'

'That's not fair and you know it!' May flared back, suddenly furious on Arthur's behalf, and that moment of defiance sealed her fate.

Incandescent with rage, Jimmy shoved her hard backwards onto the bed, then began flailing at her wildly with the leather belt he had just taken off as he undressed. Writhing in terror and agony, May twisted out of his reach but he dragged her back by her hair, struck her again viciously across her back, her scream muffled by the pillow as the leather bit cruelly into her flesh.

In that moment, panting with fright, May began to retreat into her safe place, willing herself away from the violence of the present, to somewhere pristine, peaceful, untouchable. As her body went limp, Jimmy stumbled against the bunk behind him and heard Irene whimper with fright. Turning, he stared, appalled, into the child's terrified eyes, realising with his next breath that she had seen and heard everything, everything.

'Shut your eyes,' he hissed, furiously,' shut your eyes NOW and stop that whining!'

He loomed over her and she backed up against the edge of her bed, flinching away from him in blind terror.

'Tell me you saw NOTHING!' Jimmy said, quietly now, dangerously. 'Tell me this is our secret!'

Desperately, Irene licked her dry lips and tried to muster an answer, her mind blank with fear, then clearing her throat she vomited in sheer panic all over herself, the mattress and all over Jimmy.

And then Jimmy lost his mind.

His rage consuming him utterly, he attacked her with the belt first, then his fists, his fury leaving him deaf and blind to the commotion and shouting behind him. But suddenly, he was being restrained by a man angrier than himself, a mild man whose unaccustomed emotion was rendering him strong enough to stop Jimmy's lean, hard muscles throwing punches at his tiny daughter, to throw him on to the floor and stop his assault.

Jimmy rolled away from Arthur and picked himself up off the floor, panting. May lay motionless, face down on the bed, apparently oblivious to the sickening attack she had done nothing to prevent, deaf to her daughter weeping hysterical tears as another woman swept her up into her loving, safe arms.

Lydia, Lydia who had never once held her was holding Irene now, oblivious to the vomit and the urine dripping from her nightie, hugging her fiercely against her body as she threw a look of pure loathing at Jimmy, and a contemptuous, dismissive glance at her own catatonic sister.

Lydia turned and left the room, holding her little niece against her, feeling her body quivering through their night-clothes, their hot skin connecting. Then she went down to the kitchen, put the kettle on, and gently began to bathe the little girl, washing away the hurts and stains and smells of the horror of the night, dabbing iodine on the cut where the belt buckle had caught her under her eye, and kissing her, soothing away exhausted tears with all the love she had bottled up inside her for four long years, since she lost her own child, the baby she had been powerless to save.

But this child, this child, she could save, and Lydia would do everything in her power now to make it happen.

Jimmy left that night, Arthur throwing his gear into his kit bag and escorting him briskly, firmly, out of the front door and locking it as soon as he had stepped through, then leaning his lanky body against it for a long moment to catch his breath in horror at what he had just witnessed.

He looked fearfully into the kitchen, and felt his heart turn over as he watched Lydia crooning under her breath to the trau-matised little girl, gradually calming her, soothing her to sleep in her arms.

'Do you want help carrying her upstairs?' he whispered quietly, not wanting to interrupt, to disturb the image of motherhood unfolding before his eyes.

Lydia looked up at him, her eyes gleaming with tears, and shook her head.

'I can manage,' she whispered back, 'but she's sleeping in with us tonight.'

Arthur smiled at her gently, his heart aching to see his wife's protective arms wrapped around Irene for the very first time, wishing with all his heart that he could give her her own child to care for. Then, with an effort, he forced himself to turn away and paced upstairs quietly to wake Millie, knowing that he needed her to look after May, who had not moved nor uttered a word since the attack on her and her daughter, her eyes unblinking, her back seeping blood through her dress, her face blank.

Shut away from reality.

Oblivious.

When May eventually emerged the next morning, Arthur and Millie had already left for work. She entered the kitchen quietly, then sat painfully down on a chair as Lydia turned to face her, hands on hips, an unforgiving glare on her face.

'Where's Irene?' she asked, uncertainly, wavering under the unfamiliar and frightening expression on her sister's face.

And Lydia pounced.

'Finally remembered you have a daughter, have you then?' she snapped, then softened as May's eyes filled with tears. 'She's still asleep, in our bed,' she supplied, watching her sister carefully, 'she's not up to going to school today.'

May took a deep, shuddering breath, wincing as her bruised ribs moved against the cheap material of her dressing-gown.

'Is she hurt?' she asked shakily, her eyes going to Lydia's with mute appeal.

Lydia paused, not knowing how to answer this.

'She's going to be fine,' she answered finally, 'but things are going to change around here, May. You're going to get that job back, and start bringing in some money. You need to start saving, you have to be able to support yourself without being dependent on Jimmy!'

May looked at her blankly. 'Without Jimmy?' she asked bemusedly, then looked down, understanding, blinking furiously. 'But who will look after Irene if I'm out at work?'

Lydia sighed, then looked her sister firmly in the eye.

'I will.'

May looked down at her hands furiously blinking back tears, then with an effort that cost her the world, looked up and smiled at Lydia.

'I'd better go and get ready then,' she said quietly, then as she left the room, reached out and gave her sister a sudden hug, steeling herself not to cry out in pain when Lydia unthinkingly returned the heartfelt squeeze.

Back in her room, she clutched the sink and vomited into the little porcelain basin. Once again, she stared at her ashen reflection in the cracked mirror, once again she forced her pain-wracked body into a pretty frock and buckled on her high heels.

She straightened her back as she left and walked purposefully out of the door, Lydia's grudgingly admiring gaze on her smarting shoulders as she walked briskly in the direction of her old life, her old job, another world.

Life without Jimmy? Could she really live an independent life and leave her husband? She had never even begun to contemplate such a thing, marriage was marriage, and Lydia, with her more modern ideas was far ahead of her with this line of thinking.

But, with her daughter lying in her sister's bed too wounded in body and soul to get up, her own back oozing blood into her carefully chosen red dress and the humiliation of the previous night etched in her mind, this frighteningly subversive thought lodged like a dark seed and began to take root.

Part Six

1944, Love and Loss

Stanley shipped his oars and waited, holding his breath as he listened to the sounds of the night around him. Silently, his fellow commandos did the same, all motionless, all oblivious to the burning pain in their shoulders from the long grind across the Channel, straining their ears for the sound of surf on the coast of France ahead.

They had been doing this for weeks. Rowing every other night, sleeping all day. Constantly fighting the fire of their exhausted muscles, the fear of exposure, of being caught. All painfully aware that their missions were so secret, so important that nobody would come to claim them or acknowledge their loss, their capture, their death. Their missions were that of reconnaissance, searching for landing sites, beaches they could storm, cliffs they could scale.

Night after night after night.

Stanley exhaled slowly as his ears caught the sound of the waves, and looked to his superior officer for confirmation. He nodded a curt acknowledgment with all his senses straining towards the distant coast, then gave the order to row on, those detailed for the task of readying the boat for anchoring as close to the shore as possible hunched over the bow.

When they were within spitting distance of the breakers, the order was muttered and the anchor was dropped quietly without so much as a ripple as it was let go. They all waited, the tension palpable, for the all-important depth sounding, then the line came back up with a grunted 'it's a go,' signifying that it was not too deep for the men to jump.

Without hesitation, Stanley and his men stood, slid one by one over the stern, struggling for balance against the brutal tug of the waves against their equipment, finding their feet with difficulty in the chest deep water. They struck off silently towards the shore, finding rocks underfoot, feeling their way forward in the chill dark to the foot of the cliffs above. Stanley counted his men in as he pulled himself clear of the icy water, allowed himself one searching look upwards.

Then he began to climb.

May stood outside the door of her old job, her old existence from a lifetime ago. She had had no contact with anyone since she had returned to London with Irene, burying herself in caring for her baby daughter and busying herself with the acceptable war effort for a young mother of working on the communal vegetable plots, helping to feed her own community and the country now that rationing was biting so hard. She had written to Janie once, and the reply, so full of London life and fun despite the bombing and the shortages had seemed such a world away from her new existence that she had not written back, not willing to share her secret demons and utterly unable to fill the pages with the new rhythm of her life, so removed from that of her devil-may-care friend.

Now, standing outside the door of the factory she bitterly regretted not staying in touch, desperately aware of her need for support and friendship now, more than any other time in her life. Hoping against hope that Janie would be there and would forgive her silence and welcome her with her engaging, all-encompassing grin. Grimly, May squared her shoulders and stepped across the threshold, her senses immediately flooded by the sound of the whirring machines, clattering on just as if nothing had changed from so many years before.

But everything had changed. Covering his surprise at seeing her, Mr Courtney showed her how all the girls were sewing identical material, swathes and swathes of grey silk, parachute after parachute being produced just as fast as they could sew. Explained the need for absolute secrecy, pointed out the new signs on the walls, 'Keep mum, careless talk costs lives.' Then sat her down in Mrs Hargreaves's tiny office, handing her his own voluminous handkerchief as she wept, trying to assimilate the news that Janie was dead, Janie, her fun-loving friend, Janie who pooh-poohed the air raids and slept in her own bed each night, determined not to let the war change her life, stubborn until the moment the war took that life.

When her tears had finally dried, Mr Courtney took her to a machine and explained the new task at hand. Work of absolute precision, combined with mind-numbing tedium, tempered by the knowledge that somebody else's life literally hung in the balance, that mistakes could result in a life being lost, perhaps a friend, perhaps a brother.

Perhaps a husband, thought May, fleetingly, treacherously, then forced this dark thought out of her mind as she listened to the meticulous instructions. Perfection was what was demanded, and May used this focus to clear her mind from the torment that she had experienced over the past few days, and taking a long, calming breath, she began to sew.

Millie walked back to the house, hugging her arms miserably across her chest as she approached the kitchen door. She had found the atmosphere intolerable lately, the tension from the relentless air raids and the terrifying doodlebugs fraying everyone's nerves. Seeing Lydia's new, blossoming connection with Irene warmed her heart, but at the same time, emphasised her own loneliness, her isolation from the world. The best time of the day for her now was when she went to work on the vegetable plots, the repetitive mechanical movements of her hands as she weeded giving her a kind of comfort. As each weed came free, at first she would imagine it as herself clearing the Germans out of France, out of Belgium and all the other countries she knew had fallen, but then gradually she would become aware of peace descending, her mind clearing of thought and becoming minutely focussed on the process, the order and the achievement of the unsullied earth providing her with a greater satisfaction than her earlier, angry, vicious thoughts.

As she returned home, however, the peace she had found would begin to fragment, trying to connect with the family around her that she increasingly struggled to feel a part of, but reluctant to go up to her room where Stanley's absence was ever-present.

As she walked through the kitchen door tonight though, she was immediately aware of a shift in the atmosphere, an inexplicable sea change. Irene was sitting at the table with a huge grin on her face, swinging her legs and wriggling excitedly. May was also home already, and unusually, Lydia was sitting at the table with her, not in her customary place presiding over the old stove readying the family dinner. Millie glanced questioningly at Lydia and May, then gasped as she realised another person was present, standing grinning just behind the open door.

Then faintness, confusion, crying and laughing at the same time, her tears mingling with Stanley's as he swept her up into his arms. Shocked eyes taking in his gaunt face and the dressing on the side of his head. An embarrassed but non-apologetic backwards glance as he took her hand and led her upstairs.

As he closed the bedroom door behind them, Stanley caught his breath at the sight of his young wife. Thinner, tired, but utterly beautiful, her eyes full of questions and tears of happiness.

'What's this?' she whispered, tracing his dressing with trembling fingers, but he stopped her questions with a kiss and lifted her gently but firmly onto the bed, the years of absence forgotten as they reaffirmed their love.

Afterwards, they lay quietly, drinking in the sight of each other with eyes hungry for news of the lost years, the missed time stolen from so many of their generation. Stanley told her sketchily about the injury, not a bullet, but a falling rock, a glancing blow in the dark. Millie made to question him further but he silenced her with a look, and she knew not to ask. He was all right, he said, and would be back on active service next week.

'Next week?' asked Millie, appalled, afraid to count the days remaining before they had even occurred, desperate to enjoy this precious moment with her husband of so few actual days despite the five years of marriage that bound them so deeply.

He nodded and went to speak, then stopped himself sharply.

He looked at her apologetically, desperate for her understanding.

'It's big, Millie,' he whispered, holding her close to his cheek, 'I can't tell you more but something big is going to happen and very soon.'

Millie tensed in his arms.

'I'm so afraid for you,' she replied, haltingly, and the tears fell again, this time tears of dread, fearful, helpless tears.

He held her until the storm abated. Hugged her so tightly that she could feel the leanness of his unfamiliar but yearned for body, his muscles wiry under her fingertips. His need for her.

'I'll be back, Millie,' he said, his breathing coming harshly suddenly. 'I've made it this far and I'm coming back.'

She rolled away a little so she could see his face, and gave him a long, slow smile, full of promise, full of hope, full of overwhelming love.

'Then we'd better make the most of these days then,' she replied, a flash of her old cheekiness shining through, and Stanley kissed and held her like a drowning man clinging to the rock he believed would save him.

June dawned bright and blustery. There was an upbeat feel in the air, a promise of summer and a feeling that somehow, sometime soon, surely this war must end.

The day that Stanley left, Millie walked up to the station with him, held him for one long, private moment that Arthur, seeing but not watching, knew not to disturb. Millie stood silently as the train pulled away, her eyes locked with her husband's through the sooty window, neither one willing nor able to break the contact until it was broken for them by the relentless movement of the coaches.

Then she walked away, unwilling to look for comfort despite Arthur's ready and sympathetic arms. Unable to bear human contact that wasn't Stanley. She paused momentarily at the top of the hill, her head taking her back to the house, her heart and feet taking her to the palace gardens. Finally finding the solace she needed, a silent glade, an ancient tree, a private and precious memory to treasure as the tears finally came.

Then routine and normality coming to claim her, perhaps to save her. Her job, the work on the vegetable patches, walking Irene home from school now that May was so mysteriously busy at her work and so exhausted she was barely able to function by the evening. Sitting quietly with Lydia who seemed, finally, to have found her own peace.

Each day, pushing onward. Not knowing what was coming. Not knowing that her husband was readying himself with thousands of others to turn the war around for ever. About to risk his life in the most daring, most audacious idea that could possibly have been conceived from the desperation of those dark days.

And in the morning of the sixth of June, a shout from the door roused her from her early morning torpor, made her turn from her way up the hill to look back questioningly at Lydia's excited, tearful face and run back to the house to hear the news. Hunching around the wireless with May, white-faced and silent as they listened to Churchill's' words.

As the broadcast died away, Lydia drew a long, shaky breath, then reached out and united them in a tiny circle, clutching the girls' hands as much for her own comfort as theirs.

And while they sat, all three concentrating their thoughts on the beaches in faraway France, three brothers readied themselves to launch their own attacks, their own personal best efforts to clear the Germans out of Normandy and beyond. Desperate to do their best, desperate not to let the side down. Fighting for balance in the landing craft, fighting seasickness, fighting for control. Trying not to remember another day of dying in the waves, good men lost to the elements and trapped as much by the obstacles in their path as the bullets strafing the surface of the sea around them.

United by their blood and by their cause, but separated by their regiments and the unforgiving sea, Bert, Reggie and Stanley did that most heroic act that could be asked of a person – overcame their fear and ran, unflinching and unhesitating, towards the guns on the beach, their black snub barrels spitting death and destruction at the swarms of men spewing from the waves.

And hundreds of miles away, the Eighth Army and Jimmy paused for breath, gathering strength for the last push to liberate Rome.

And the girls, those girls whose lives had been dictated to and shaped by this war and the last, hugged each other fiercely, then stoically and steadily walked their separate ways to do their own, quiet duty.

It was the longest day.

A day when May sat at her sewing machine, different material placed before her but seeing the parachutes of the past weeks floating down through the skies into a French dawn in her mind's eye. Millions of stitches, thousands upon thousands of men, every one dependent upon the other.

A day when her thoughts rested with her brothers, her mind racing and her heart searching to feel them through time and space, hoping to send them courage when they needed it most. Wishing she could have an inkling of what they faced today, but afraid to face it at the same time, grateful suddenly for the hated black lines of censure that had protected her and her family up until now, Churchill's words of truth this morning piercing their little bubble of existence like a sudden, shocking shard of glass.

She jumped violently, disturbed from her reverie by the gentle touch of a hand on her shoulder. Startled, she turned to see Mr Courtney standing smiling at her compassionately.

'I'm sorry, sir,' she stuttered, horrified to be found wanting, then paused as the smile disappeared from his kindly face.

'No need to be sorry,' he murmured, quietly, 'I think the whole world is holding its breath today. 'Do you know where your husband is?' he asked then, watching her face carefully and seeing it snap shut at the mention of Jimmy.

'Italy, I think,' she answered brusquely, looking down at the machine at her table, 'but my brothers are all in France.'

Her eyes filled suddenly with tears, and she turned abruptly away from him. Mr Courtney watched her for a moment longer, saw her gathering her reserve around her like a cloak.

'I know what Jimmy did to you,' he blurted suddenly, then hesitated as May raised a horrified face to his. 'Janie told me about your scars,' he muttered, shocked by the sudden fury in her eyes, wishing he had never started these words, but at the same time wanting to reach out to this enigma of a young woman, as fragile as a kitten yet full of grit and pride. May met his gaze and glared at him until he looked away.

'It was none of Janie's business and it's certainly none of yours,' she returned, tartly, then dismissed him sharply by pressing her foot to the pedal and letting the fresh new material whir beneath her fingers.

Later, she paused for a moment, letting her mind wander to his words and obvious concern for her. His regard for her had clearly increased of late, she was often called upon for the more demanding and difficult tasks, from training the endless new girls through to precision tailoring for those wealthy clients who stayed safe and grew rich from the war. She had spent more time in his company, and had come to value his warm words of praise and his appreciation of his work.

She stopped then, testing an idea at the edge of her consciousness. Could it be more than just professional appreciation? Was he becoming interested in her as a woman? May shook her head and gave a tiny, self-deprecating laugh. Ridiculous to even think of it, she chided herself, then realised that dismissing the thought made her sad. She shook her head again and wiped furiously at her eyes to stop the unforgivable sin of allowing tears to fall on the fresh material before her.

And suddenly he was there beside her again, reaching across, just as he had when he told her that Janie had died, holding out a silk handkerchief, clearing his throat gruffly as he looked away to give her time to collect herself.

'Penny for your thoughts,' he asked quietly, looking searchingly at her after a long moment.

'Well they're not about Jimmy!' she exploded suddenly, defiantly, then stopped herself before she went too far, her throat working furiously to contain the words threatening to spill forth.

Mr Courtney nodded, silently. 'I know,' he said. 'I didn't think that they would be. Go home, May. I know you need to be with your family while your brothers are out there today. Go now.'

May looked at him tremulously, gratefully, then smiled, a rare beam of sunlight on this dark and fearful day, stood and left without looking back.

Afraid to look back. Afraid suddenly of what those rare words of kindness had meant to her and just how much he had touched her. A smile daring to break through as she turned towards Alexandra Palace, Muswell Hill, and home.

The news trickled in from France. Incredulous, London held its breath, scarcely daring to believe the tide had changed, that they could sleep in their beds instead of retreating to the shelters every night, cheek by jowl to brave it through another night of howling, crushing destruction. Night after night of listening to that heart-stopping silence as the doodlebug engines cut out to deal their deadly blows to the sitting ducks below, years beyond being buoyed up by propaganda, no longer cheered by the wireless chirping its well-worn positivity in the harsh light of yet another broken, rubble-strewn dawn.

Arthur and the girls worked, waited and hoped. 'No news is good news,' they told themselves briskly every morning, each avoiding one another's eyes as they waited for a letter, hoping against hope that a telegram would not come first.

May's letter came first. Jubilant, the Eighth Army pushing through the hills of Italy, sweeping a wave of hope through Europe. The first optimism in years, the Italians rushing to support the Allies with all the conviction and fervour of the recently converted.

May stuffed the letter grimly into her handbag and put a little more of her savings away each week. Irene looked at her face and studiously avoided asking for news of her father. Her mother's daughter, she had not mentioned him again after that last terrible night, choosing to efface his memory as surely as May had effaced her own sensibilities to survive.

Lydia collected two letters on the same day, Reggie and Bert were safe for the moment, but were marching towards Germany quickly, the Allies not daring to lose the momentum of that first almighty push onto the beaches of Normandy.

But nothing came for Millie. She paced each morning, trying not to stare out of the window to the street below, trying not to let her desperation break through. A painful, long-forgotten memory twisted in Lydia's heart as she watched her usually bubbly sister-in-law's face grow whiter and more pinched with each passing day – the memory of her dead sister Edie, waiting for Edward to return from the Great War, along with all the other survivors of that war which did not end all wars, she thought bitterly, scrubbing the step outside the shop with a renewed viciousness, not even for the briefest reprieve of one single generation.

Then Reggie wrote again. He had seen Stanley. Millie broke down and wept at last, ragged sobs tearing from her throat as she heard that he was alive. That his special commandos unit had been asked to volunteer for the Burma campaign, a desperate bid to halt the seemingly unstoppable Japanese army and win the war in the East.

That he had gone without telling her.

Lydia watched with increasing dismay as Millie closed down, drawing herself inward to survive her very private pain. She wished she could tell her how much she missed her brother, how often she would catch her breath as she remembered Stanley and May sitting giggling together on their mother's lap, identical shocks of black curls shaking with laughter at some shared joke, their twin bond rendering them seemingly inseparable. She wished she could reach out and smooth away some of her pain, but each time she tried to reach her, Millie withdrew further, unable to accept comfort, unable to comprehend why Stanley would have gone so far from her without a word. She could not feel her connection with him anymore, and, as it broke her heart, Lydia watched sorrowfully, searching for a chance to offer solace to her much-loved friend.

Guiltily, Lydia revelled in the time she spent with Irene, and found a new and peculiar delight in telling her all about her brave uncle, met only once and gone before she could truly know him. Irene loved to hear the tales, especially when Lydia told her about the nightly rowing expeditions, Millie having told them about this quietly, and with oh such pride in her voice during the aftermath of Operation Overlord. Stanley, Irene's mysterious uncle, swiftly became a heroic figure of derring-do, and the barren auntie and the little girl became ever closer during the tales of his half-imagined, half-real exploits, Irene curled up on a kitchen chair listening intently as Lydia talked, a figure of perpetual motion as she cooked, chopped, and spun the yarns that were rapidly becoming ingrained in their family folklore.

May began to talk about Stanley too, but she chose to talk to Mr Courtney.

They had grown closer.

She began to tell him about her daughter and her family, about her brothers scattered across the war-torn world. She talked as she worked, never raising her eyes from her machine, sublimely unaware of his eyes resting on the nape of her neck and the curve of her cheek as she leaned over her work.

May was now his most accomplished seamstress, her natural eye for drape and texture and form combined with a meticulous attention to the fine detail of intricate stitching making her stand out from the crowd. More often than not choosing to sew the tiniest of stitches by hand, striving for and achieving greater finesse than the machine could offer. A flair for sketching new designs sudden surfacing, exciting him with her visions of an elegant future beyond the realms of rationing and recycled material. Her creation of a wedding dress for a client made from swathes of grey parachute silk making the front page of the London papers and putting his business up there into the bright lights of fashion in a happier, more upbeat London than any of them could begin to recall.

The day that May heard her brother had gone to Burma, Mr Courtney saw her pale drawn face, and felt his heart twist painfully in his chest. He sat quietly at his desk, determinedly trying to analyse his feelings in a way that was entirely customary for him. He rarely acted impulsively, tending more habitually towards thinking deeply and seriously, to puzzle it all out to his own satisfaction before he chose to react to any new situation.

This was utterly, profoundly different. He had begun to glimpse that his feelings for May were not open to analysis, and could not be strictly rationalised according to his usual protocol.

He loved her.

He loved every inch of her married, motherly body. He loved every pore of her skin, yearned to kiss away the bitter scars of a deeper anger, a darker force than he had ever encountered, wanted to take her for himself and help her, love her, heal her.

'Mr Courtney?' A timid voice disturbed his reverie, and he ducked his face down to take a physical hold of his feelings, then looked straight up into the eyes of the woman he had just been dreaming of. A woman who smiled at him and made his heart glow with warmth.

A woman whom he was quite convinced was utterly unaware of his turmoil.

Taking a deep breath, he forced himself to return to business, smiled brightly and began to discuss the day's work, his breezy tone forcibly chasing away the passion of his thoughts. Deliberately distancing himself from the young woman he had only just realised he had loved for years, a mother married to a soldier, a man Mr Courtney knew, as surely as he knew his own heart, had hurt her badly.

Puzzled, May withdrew carefully as soon as she could, feeling she had intruded on him, misread what she had thought was a need to talk on his part. Sitting at her workstation, confused and confusing thoughts chasing through her mind, loneliness creeping up on her like a London pea-souper, threatening to swamp and engulf her in its darkness.

When she left that evening, Mr Courtney shut the door with a heavy heart, put his head in his hands, and wept.

The letter finally came for Millie. Arthur met the postboy as he left that morning, intercepted it for one fearful moment, then turned and gave it to his sister-in-law, watching her clamp down hard on her feelings long enough to dash up the stairs to read it in much needed privacy.

She sat on the edge of their bed, the bed whose shared nights of their five-year marriage she could count on the fingers of her hands. Her hands shook as she opened the letter, eyes scanning desperately through the harsh black lines of censure to decipher what her young husband had tried so hard to convey to his desolate and bereft wife.

My dearest Millie,

I must ask you to forgive me, sweetheart, I should have written sooner but we were taken so swiftly from France to this campaign that there was so little time. I saw Reggie and he told me he would tell you I was all right, I hope you got the message from him.

We all got through storming the beaches, Millie, I don't know how, but we did. I hope to tell you about it one day after all this is over but I need to do that face to face, it doesn't bear describing in a letter. I haven't seen Bert but Reggie knew he'd got through, I think they are both headed towards Germany now.

But I have to tell you about me. I volunteered for the Burma Campaign. I know you'll think I'm mad, that everyone at home probably wonders why I'd do this when the end is in sight, with Hitler on the run.

It's because it won't be over unless we finish it, Millie. It isn't just Germany, is it? The Japs are everywhere, they're just swarming over anywhere and everywhere they take a fancy to, just like Hitler did in Europe.

We used to call the Great War ' the war to end all wars.' Well it didn't, did it? And that's because we didn't finish it, we let the Germans off too lightly, we let them build up and do it all over again. I held a man in my arms while he died at Dunkirk, and Millie, he should have married my sister and he should have been able to enjoy a life with her. And what he actually got was the same deal all over again, only this time he didn't make it through.

I know it seems remote to everyone back in London, love, but it's not, love, not really. They are killing Brits in Singapore, in Malaya, everywhere they rest their greedy eyes, and, Millie, they have been doing it since the beginning, while our eyes were on Hitler. We have to stop them, Millie, and they need commandos, it's not easy terrain like we had in France. I had *to volunteer, for Edward's sake and for all of us, really I did or it would all have been pointless, just like the last war.*

I'm all right, love. I feel very tired all the time, I think it's maybe the heat but really I think it started with all the rowing before Operation Overlord, I really think that took it out of me. My shoulders still ache, I wish you could rub them for me like you did when I came home!

I miss you, love. I hope this is over soon, over properly, so I can come back home with my head high and sweep you off your feet. I want to start a family, Millie, I want to have a home with you and lead a quiet life again, do you remember how you used to scrub the step of the shop while I was cashing up for the day? I used to love that.

I'm sorry I couldn't write sooner, love. I hope you understand why I had to volunteer and forgive me for it.

Every night I look at a little sketch I made of you years ago and smile as I fall asleep with you in my mind. I hope you are safe, sweetheart, more than anything else. Look after yourself, love, and please, please stay safe.

All my love, as ever,
Your Stanley

Tucked inside the tightly folded paper, Millie felt another thin sheet, unfolded it gently as her tears finally began to fall. A tiny sketch of a rug, a picnic basket, a pair of discarded high heels and an oak tree. A place more dear to her than anywhere, the place where she had fallen in love with this brave, serious, thoughtful man she was so proud to call her husband.

A man who was now fighting in a jungle to keep her safe, thousands of miles and a world away, in a war whose ferocity and rage she could scarcely imagine nor begin to understand.

After that, nothing. No letters from the boys, no word from any of them.

For months and months.

The misery of the air raids had begun again, but this time it felt worse somehow, the new, terrifying V2 rockets, which would simply explode and destroy half of a street without a moment's warning, began to beat the last of the resilience out of London.

Arthur and the girls took each day as it came, getting up and going to work, not daring to wonder what could be happening out there to their loved ones cast unwittingly upon the world stage. Child soldiers, utterly unknowing what they had signed up for so many years before, the enthusiasm and valour of youth and optimism surely spent after so many bitter years of warfare. The end that they all thought was coming suddenly seemed unattainable, a fool's dream, just like the 'home by Christmas' war of so long ago it hurt to remember.

The news from the East was grim, the Japanese seeming to spread like a cancer across countries whose names, once unknown, were now synonymous with atrocities in every Londoner's mind.

May took her work over to Mr Courtney that morning, wanting to discuss her new idea for the eye-catching design that always held centre stage in the shop window of the designer shop front. She held a sketch in her hand, and seeing this, Mr Courtney immediately ushered her through into the privacy of Mrs Hargreave's office, allowing them a chance to discuss new designs without being overheard.

'It's almost as serious as keeping mum,' joked May, then fell silent as she saw the intense expression on his face. 'What's wrong, Mr Courtney?' she faltered, then smiled as he grinned at her, chiding her as ever to call him 'George'.

'I'll call you George in here,' she conceded, 'but not out there on the shop floor, the girls will tear me to pieces for sucking up to the boss!'

He smiled triumphantly and leant over her shoulder to look at her sketch, the flowing lines catching the idea of her intent so accurately that her talent made him shake his head admiringly.

And in the blink of an eye, everything changed. May became acutely aware of him, his fresh scent, the warmth emanating from his cheek, suddenly, inexplicably so close to hers. Her skin tingled in unwitting response, and infinitesimally, she swayed towards him.

And then he did something so out of character that neither could react for one long, heart-stopping moment.

The angle of her jaw and the curve of her eyelashes on her cheek as she looked at the drawing utterly overwhelmed him, overcame his analytical nature and his customary reserve. George Courtney finally surrendered to the moment and kissed her.

May walked home later in a daze. Happy. Happy in a way she could not truly remember, or perhaps had never even experienced before. The gentleness and tenderness of his touch filling her heart, the raw passion she had felt with Jimmy eclipsed by a new, deep calm. She didn't notice anyone around her as she walked up the hill, didn't notice how passers-by smiled at the sight of a young woman clearly lost in a dream.

She did notice, though, the fact that the front door was ajar. The front door, never used, all visitors doing what was normal in their street and going around the back to rap on the kitchen door.

All visitors except the postman.

She hesitated for the space of a heartbeat, then dashed up the steps to the open door as fast as her shaking legs would take her, legs that had suddenly turned to jelly and felt like they might let her down.

When she saw Millie, kneeling on the floor, rocking back and forth silently, the telegram clutched in her bloodless hand, her legs did finally let her down. Her new found joy and her customary veneer of resilience deserted her as she read of her brother's death, her twin, her soul mate, dead in a jungle in a foreign land. Not dead from a bullet or a bomb, but dead from leukaemia, leaching the strength from his body as surely as the war had leached the strength from the generation that had fought it. Dead from a disease he had not guessed at, blaming his exhaustion on his night raids, his head injury, battle fatigue.

Dead, nonetheless.

Irene, arriving home later with Lydia, would never forget nor could understand until many years later why her mother raged through the house, tearing at her hair and weeping that they had got the wrong one, that the wrong man had been taken, the wrong man had died. Watching her Auntie Millie whimpering, sitting rocking back and forth, clutching at her sunken little stomach and saying over and over that she had nothing, that she had lost everything, that she had no part of Stanley left for her at all. Slinking up to bed to escape the shock of seeing adults break down, the adults that until now had shielded her and protected her as best they could from the mad world into which she had been born.

Finally in private, finally able at last to weep hot, childish tears for the uncle she had begun to turn into a hero but had never really known.

George Courtney saw the change in May as soon as she walked through the door the following week. May had gone absent, disappearing from work without a word, and he could only surmise that she was avoiding him, regretting their kiss and sudden intimacy of that precious moment, so precious to him that he had paced the floorboards for a week, ceaselessly and relentlessly berating himself for being too presumptuous, for frightening her away.

But when she raised her exhausted, ashen face to his and smiled, a ray of hope broke through his dark thoughts and he smiled back, tentatively, then more broadly as she followed him determinedly to the back office and closed the door behind her, oblivious to the curious looks from the girls on the machines.

Then opened his arms to her as he saw the tears starting in her eyes, and held her while she wept anew and told him of her brother, the brother she had been so proud of, the twin who had known her better than anyone and who was now lost to her.

A letter had come from Reggie following those dark days after the telegram had come and delivered the news that had struck at the hearts of the beleaguered little family, slowly succumbing to the exhaustion of endless war. A letter that gave some scant comfort to Millie who wept afresh at the kindness emanating from the page.

Unbeknown to any of them, Reggie had been posted to India six weeks beforehand, the lack of news that had worried Lydia so not due to a push towards Germany where Bert was marching, but due to the long and unguessed-at passage by sea.

He had been told of Stanley's illness through an officer recently arrived from Burma, and immediately applied for special dispensation to travel overland to be with him. Their shared credentials of serving since '39 right through to storming the beaches at D-

Day swung it for him, and he had made the bone-rattling, weary trip by train in time to hold his little brother's hand as he died, and to shed tears for him by his dusty grave.

George listened quietly as May talked, holding her close and feeling her tears soaking his shirt. His love for her filled his heart, silenced him with the depth of his emotion. When she finally stopped talking and her sobs had died away, he looked down at her face and kissed her gently, smoothing the tears away from her eyes with his thumbs.

'I want to look after you,' he murmured tenderly, and felt a rush of pure joy as May shut her eyes and leaned into his embrace, allowing him to hold her and soothe her aching soul. Then, suddenly unable to help himself, 'May would you leave him? Would you leave Jimmy and come with me?'

The wireless finally crackled and fell silent, the words of Winston Churchill still ringing in her ears. The war in Europe was over, and the boys were coming home. May sat staring blindly into the fire, twisting the diamond ring she had once loved so much endlessly around her finger as she thought of what the news meant to her, what fate now lay in store for her and her little girl.

Which fate she might choose, for she did indeed have a choice.

Years before, so long ago that she barely recognised the memory now, Jimmy's love and her ability to inflame and then calm him had felt like a whole new world. She had felt the power every girl feels as she becomes a woman, and she had taken that great leap of faith required to commit to love.

She had been ready to stretch her wings and fly, fly with Jimmy.

And now, on this dark night so many, many years later, twisting her beautiful ring as if she were trying to twist it off her work-worn finger, how could she presume to dream of another man?

Another man, while that volatile, unpredictable, exciting and frightening man she called her husband and the father of her daughter had been out there, fighting for their safety, fighting to end this desperate war they had never understood nor dreamed of six interminable years ago.

Another man who loved her, accepted her as she was, didn't put her onto an unattainable pedestal and beat her as she fell. Another man who loved her gently, completely, realistically.

The words of the radio and the girls at work ringing in her ears... 'Get ready, your soldier boy is coming home! Make sure you are there to look after him. He's been looking after you and England for years. Now it's your turn.'

Get ready to do your duty and look after him now as your hero returns.

Hero.

Notwithstanding.

No escape.

May had suffered a desperate birth alone. She had learned to survive whippings and beatings. She had learned to go out to work while her sister cared for her child. She had sheltered that tiny child from the mind-numbing fear of the doodlebug's engine cutting out, knowing it was falling nearby and that nothing could survive a direct hit, then for the past few, long months, the spontaneous eruptions and destruction caused by the silent V2s. She had had to find the courage to tell her daughter that all her school-friends were dead, killed by just such a direct hit during a birthday party that Irene had been too ill to attend, burning up with measles and spared the bomb but left bereft and friendless in her childish world.

But nothing she had ever learned could have prepared her for the day she told George she was taking Jimmy back.

That their dream was over before it had begun to take root.

She walks through the crowds the next morning to work, the clicking of her high heels on the pavement ticking in her mind like a time-bomb, and it seems to her that no one else in London has any intention of working. Hordes of people laughing, hugging each other, dancing in the streets, some of them clearly not gone home since last night after the announcement they have waited so long to hear. It seems to her that the world is happy again, has forgotten all the pain and the loss of the past, nightmarish, war-torn years.

But for May, the pain is not over. The pain is to come.

George is waiting for her when she arrives, smiling ruefully when she raises her eyebrows at the deserted factory floor, the silence of the machines hanging over them like a shroud.

For the first time, they are alone. And for the first time, May walks without hesitation into his open arms, allows herself, just for the space of a single heartbeat, to feel the love radiating from this kind, caring man.

Before she pulls away.

Before she tells him, blurting out as fast as she is able, the words tumbling out relentlessly so as not to give herself a chance to change her mind. Watching his face fall, bitter disappointment giving way to abject misery as his dream shrivels and dies.

Then she walks out of the door, walking blindly back to Muswell Hill, the tears shielding her from the revellers crowding around her, the crowd parting but giving her curious looks as she passes through, oblivious. She stops at the house, suddenly unable to enter. Unable to bear the kindness, the understanding and the comfort she knows her family will offer. Walking past and up the hill, up, up to Alexandra Palace. Finally falling to her knees on the damp ground, rubbing the heel of her hand back and forth over the deep pain in her breast, her body convulsing with harsh, wrenching sobs barely yards away from the place where, a lifetime ago, her dead brother had loved with all his heart.

Loved and lost, another indirect casualty of this war that had taken so many lives, so many loves.

Victory in Europe.

All over.

Part Seven

1950, Moving On

Many years later, Irene would find it hard to remember the sequence of events after her father returned from the war, exhausted by his long journey across war-torn Europe. The night that he arrived, darkened from the sun and full of even darker passion for his young wife, bitter resentment seething from both father and daughter alike when he realised Irene was still sharing the room she had always shared with her mother, who had not had the foresight to realise that it might have been politic to move her in with Millie for a little while. The sudden move from Muswell Hill to the little flat in Hornsey Rise Gardens, the loneliness of separation from Lydia, Lydia who had become her second mother and just as important a part of her life as May had ever been. Millie's sad eyes as the little family broke apart in Jimmy's quest for freedom and independence, May scurrying along in his wake trying, as ever, to please and appease.

Her Uncle Bert, a complete stranger to her, walking in and sitting down at the table as if he had never left, and heading off to the pub just as soon as it was open just like he had before the war. Reggie, another unknown uncle, but in her mother's eyes thinner, immeasurably older and haunted by the sights he had seen in the push to liberate Europe, then the shocking images of torture he had witnessed when fighting the Japanese in Burma. Dear, dear Reggie, the one who walked through the door and swept Millie into his arms, whispering quietly how sorry he was about Stanley and held her as she wept anew, the tears never truly far from the surface since the first news of her loss.

Her mother leaving her job with no word of explanation and starting afresh with a new factory producing cheap dresses to buy 'off the peg,' without individual tailoring, something that she had always scorned in the past.

Both mother and daughter walking on eggshells around the brooding, volatile man who could not settle nor hold down a job, who did not seem to know what he needed to be happy. Waiting for his next explosion, wondering who would be hurt the most.

Worst of all, listening to her mother weeping in the tiny kitchen late at night when she thought everyone was asleep, clutching a cushion to her breast and trying to stifle her sobs with the corner pressed to her mouth.

Night after night after night.

What Irene could never forget though, however much she might try, was the day that her world as she knew it fell apart.

The day began as every day did in the little flat which had never once felt like home. In fact, ironically, now that she was ten, five full years since the war had ended, her fondest memories and thoughts of 'home' that remained were the nights snuggled between her mother and Millie in the Anderson shelter, with Arthur and Lydia curled up on the other side but all within reach of a ready hug and a kiss goodnight.

Irene sat silently at the kitchen table, chewing manfully and trying her hardest to swallow the toast that her mother had made her for breakfast, what should have been a favourite turning to dust in her dry mouth. Jimmy sat drumming his fingers on the table, while May flicked a tea towel nervously around, drying up and putting plates away as quietly as she could so as not to make a clatter.

'What time do you need to go, Jimmy?' she asked eventually, watching his face anxiously as she spoke, and Irene dared to glance up at her father to hear the answer.

'I need to report to the foreman at eight,' he replied, glancing irritably at Irene who had begun to splutter as the toast caught in her throat, desperately trying to wash it down with her glass of water before she drew too much attention to herself. She had become very good at that, thought May, sadly, her beautiful, vibrant daughter had become a pale little shadow of her previously animated self, choosing to merge with the background instead of holding the limelight like she used to, like May herself used to, she conceded wistfully.

Like mother, like daughter.

Jimmy was starting at a new job today, and May was trying her best to keep the atmosphere light, to smooth over any hint of tension before he left. She needed him to find work, and desperately. The lack of money was the least of her problems, what she needed was her husband to find some focus, to get out of the house instead of pacing like a caged tiger ready to lash out at the first person who came within reach of his claws.

Each and every job that he'd taken over the past five years had gone the same way, Jimmy, unable to settle since his days as a soldier, unable to take discipline from anyone in peacetime, unable to knuckle under and do as he was told. Each time, fired within days, coming home to vent his fury on May, who would flinch as he slammed through the door, the truth of the situation plain to see on his bitter, angry face, the rage bursting out as soon as he caught sight of her sympathetic but wary expression.

The welts on her back would open as soon as he hit her, never even beginning to heal from the last onslaught. Blood oozing, tears running.

All in stubborn silence. Escaping, as she had learned so early in their stormy marriage, simply by withdrawing from an unacceptable reality. Not dreaming of what she might have lost, not remembering a love that might have flourished. Just silent, blank nothingness until she would slowly become aware that the physical onslaught had ceased and that Jimmy's rage had again collapsed into pathetic self-pity and regret.

Today of all days, however, May felt her breath catch in her throat as she dared to entertain a little ray of hope. This job would be outside, not cooped up, working as part of a team but each his own cog in the wheel. Interdependent, but with no rigid hierarchy, this simple labouring job seemed to offer a solution to Jimmy's frustration and pent-up resentment of anyone who dared issue him with an order, dared take away his new-found autonomy that, in truth, sat ill with his civilian clothes.

Irene managed to stop coughing and again sat in self-effacing silence, concentrating on finishing her breakfast without incident. As soon as she was decently able, she meant to slip out of the door and off to school, and, dutifully kissing her father goodbye, she gave her mother a heartfelt squeeze as she went to pick up her battered leather satchel.

Then Jimmy left too, May leaning in weak-kneed relief against the sink as she saw him striding briskly down the road towards the bus stop. Please God let this one work out, she prayed silently, squeezing her eyes shut against the images of the past few months of boom and bust, hope and despair.

Then she pulled herself together and left the flat too, rushing to her own work, ready to focus on her meticulous sewing which no one seemed to appreciate anymore now that the emphasis was more about volume of production rather than quality of the garment she was working on. The cheap, bright materials slipping through her fingers to be swallowed by her hungry machine, the rhythm soothing her thoughts, lulling her into some kind of peace. Her mind rigidly on the task, steadfastly refusing to look back on her old job where she had found so much satisfaction, so much comfort and – she clamped her lips shut tightly – oh, so much love.

At five o'clock, she stood, stretched her aching back and went to have her card stamped before she walked out the door, taking deep breaths of fresh air in the chilly autumn evening as she turned dutifully for home.

Irene was already there, sitting at the table in the little kitchen quietly sketching in the treasured little pad Lydia had given her for her birthday. Her mother's talent for catching line and form, as well as Stanley's eye for clarity had clearly been passed on to Irene, and May glanced proudly at the top page as her daughter stood to coax the gas stove into boiling a kettle for the cup of tea they always enjoyed together before Jimmy would arrive home, threatening their fragile peace with his unpredictable presence.

They sat, sipping and chatting peaceably, Irene trying to ignore the fact that her mother's eye was always on the clock. Time to get the dinner on, time to spruce herself up to please Jimmy. He always liked it when she made an effort, and although her eyes stung from her fine stitching and her back ached from sitting for so many hours, May splashed her face grimly and painted on a fresh smile to greet him when he walked through the door.

But Jimmy didn't come.

The clock ticked on relentlessly, and as the tension became palpable, both May and Irene turned to other tasks once they had put his dinner into the oven to keep it warm, both acknowledging without words that he should have been home by now. Both wondering fearfully what was keeping him, and what his mood would be like when he finally returned. At nine, May looked at Irene, her heart going out to her as she saw her fingers shaking as she fiddled with a loose curl that she was tugging at over and over. Impulsively she reached out and tucked the stray curl behind her ear, giving her a sudden hug.

'Go to bed, lovey,' she said quietly, but Irene shook her head and pushed her away, irritably, 'Mum, I want to stay up and keep you company,' knowing that what she was really saying was 'safety in numbers'.

And in that moment, the door burst open.

Jimmy stood, swaying in the doorway, and May's heart lurched with fear as she realised instantly how drunk he was.

'Go to bed Irene, right now!' she hissed, and Irene backed away quickly, suddenly too afraid to stay. Scuttling into her room, but then creeping back to listen at the kitchen door, desperately wanting to hide but needing to be near her mother, wanting to protect her.

May drew herself up and smiled brightly, steeled herself to ask,

'How did it go today, Jimmy?' To her surprise, he smiled at her then, caught her by the waist and spun her round before putting her back down, grabbing the table to catch her breath.

'What happened? Did you like it?' she asked, scarcely daring to believe that it had all worked out this time, just when they so desperately needed it.

'Ah no, it really wasn't my thing at all,' replied Jimmy dismissively, pulling away from her and dropping his eyes furtively from her questioning gaze, 'the boss was an idiot and I told him so! But May, listen to me, I've had a much better idea, a new plan for us all!'

Before she could stop herself, May sighed heavily, and in that moment, Jimmy exploded.

'How dare you!' he yelled in her face, shoving her hard backwards so that she half fell across the table, her hands scrabbling frantically at his chest to try to hold him away, but it was no use, his fingers twisted viciously in her hair and he slapped her face with his free hand, his eyes glistening with rage inches from her own. May held his gaze for a moment, feeling the terror turning her insides to liquid, the fear visceral within her.

And then, like a tiny avenging angel, Irene stepped through the kitchen door, her face white but her eyes blazing with hatred.

'Let go of her!' she screamed shrilly, and Jimmy laughed, laughed in the face of his little daughter, and slapped her mother again hard, her head snapping back then lolling on her slender neck, shocking red blood starting from her lip.

And then the temper that had been borne into Irene erupted. She hurled herself at her father, clawing at his face with her nails and biting, kicking, flailing at him with everything that she could muster, the fury within fuelled by the derisive laughter ringing in her ears, mocking her as he picked her up and threw her bodily across the table. In that instant the teapot shattered, spilling cold stale tea across the scrubbed wood, spreading towards her precious sketch book, and gasping, she twisted free of Jimmy's hands to snatch it up out of harm's way. Betraying to him in that defensive movement how important it was to her, how many hours of precise and loving pencil strokes were contained within, allowing him to see a chink in her armour. Her eyes leaking bitter, bitter tears as he snatched it from her grasp and shredded the pages one by one, dropping them into the puddle forming on the lino on the floor, her hands pressed firmly against her mouth to suppress the harsh sobs rising in her throat.

And all the while, her mother standing there, frozen still and bleeding, watching the scene through dull, destroyed eyes. Not moving to stop him, not trying to save her daughter's most precious treasure.

Then her father reaching into the breast pocket of his jacket, throwing down a bulky envelope before them.

'Tickets for us all,' he announced, triumphantly. 'So you think I can't provide for you, is that right, May? Well now you've got another think coming. Tickets for Australia. Just the three of us. Work for everyone, no more rationing, as much food as we can eat. We leave at the end of the month.'

Then yawning silence as Irene turned and crept from the room.

The night before they were due to leave, May went over to the big house on Muswell Hill with Irene to spend a last, precious evening with her family. At the last minute, she wondered guiltily whether she should invite Jimmy, but he had other plans to go drinking with some old mates and Irene's pinched, imploring little face stopped her from trying to change his mind.

Irene clutched her hand as they went round the back to rap on the kitchen door and walk in, the familiar warmth enveloping them as soon as they stepped inside.

Lydia turned from the stove where dinner was cooking and smiled, taking the few steps across the room to sweep Irene up for a cuddle, her eyes fixed on her sister's over her shoulder.

'Are you all right?' she mouthed quietly, and May nodded, her eyes immediately filling with tears and belying her action. Lydia winced sympathetically and pulled May into her embrace, all three hugging tightly without the need for words.

'I've cooked,' announced Lydia, rather unnecessarily, and May kissed her cheek.

'Thank you, Lyd,' she replied, 'I just want to be here with all of you tonight, I didn't fancy going out at all.' She glanced down at Irene and said, 'Why don't you pop up to Millie's room, love, and tell her we're here?'

Irene scampered gratefully up the stairs and May turned again, back into Lydia's now teary embrace.

'What am I going to do without you, Lyd?' she asked, desperately, and somehow, Lydia reached deep inside herself once again to nurture her with all the love and strength that her mother would have done had she lived to see this day.

'It's a new start, May. You have to try and make the best of it, maybe this is what you all need?' she offered, her eyes never leaving May's as she spoke.

May looked away and dashed the tears from her face as she did so.

'You're right,' she said, firmly. 'I just have to get on with it and make it work. For all of us. And Lydia, I will write, I promise. And I will find out how to book calls and telephone you, I really will!'

And one by one, Reg, Bert, Arthur and Millie joined them in

the kitchen, passing Irene from lap to lap as they ate and talked and held each other within the little cocoon of that family kitchen's warmth, all aware of and connected by the love amongst them that had sustained them all through the hardest of times and would seem destined to do so for many more times to come.

May leant back in her chair, watching them and feeling her heart go out to each and every one of them. Trying to let her heart swell with love without allowing it to break. Imprinting them all in her memory to sustain her for the unknown ahead of her, to help her forge through with her daughter to embrace and survive in a strange new world.

The other side of the world.

The next day, Millie felt the treacherous tears prickling at the back of her eyes again, took a deep breath and tried to steady herself against the overpowering emotions threatening to swamp her. With a rueful glance in the mirror, she picked up her handbag and straightened her jacket, taking one last moment to get a grip on herself before walking downstairs to the kitchen where Arthur and Lydia were waiting for her.

Waiting to say goodbye to a woman who had been a child to Lydia then a sister, a woman who had picked herself up again and again, struggling against the odds to make a happy life for the little girl who had touched and brightened all of their lives. May had given them Irene, and Irene had held them together in so many ways during the war years, given them all a reason to get up every grim and lonely day, a reason to fight and keep the world safe. A lifeline for Lydia, helping her to reconnect with her maternal instinct and allowing herself to heal and recover from that terrible day which had blighted and almost taken her life.

The child who would creep into Millie's bed and stroke her tears away when she woke to hear her weeping in the night as she lay and mourned Stanley, a little glow of love who would snuggle against her aunt and press close to her heart until the sobs would slowly subside.

So many times.

The thought of saying goodbye today froze Millie's heart and made her skinny frame, which had never put the weight back on since the worst of the war years, shiver with a trepidation worse than anything she had ever felt in the Blitz. Laying eyes on her ashen-faced sister-in-law, however, she smiled bravely and went to take her hands.

'Lydia, she'll be all right,' she said brightly, with a firmness she could not feel. 'No rations, just imagine!'

Even Lydia had to smile at that, just as Millie had hoped, and Arthur sent her a ghost of a smile, grateful for her support on this day, this day that felt so much like a funeral.

Walking up to the station together, unable to talk. Seeing the taxi cab pull up, Jimmy jumping out to unload the three brown trunks, containing everything a family could be allowed to begin a new life on the other side of the world. Three little trunks. Three lives departing.

A choking sob caught in Millie's throat, and she made to lean for a moment against Arthur, but he was already gone, stepping forward to snatch Irene up in his arms in a whirl of tears and laughter, and it was Reggie who caught her arm and steadied her, slipping his arm around her shoulders to give her the support she so badly needed. And so, so, missed.

May clutching at Lydia, the two of them rocking in a silent, desperate embrace. No words, nothing more to say. Lydia's hands snarled in Irene's curls, caught up as if they could never be separated, the little girl wrapping herself around her auntie in a way she had before once long ago, on a long dark night when they had both needed each other for rescue.

A blur of faces, a smudge of tears. Then just simply silence, the little family standing bereft, no child to lighten the mood or brighten their lives, no future to envisage or dream of together, Irene, their collective war baby, their only chance of a new generation, gone. Gone.

Walking back to the house and into the kitchen, a vision of normality shattered by a scene Millie had never dreamt she would ever see. Lydia, Lydia the lynch pin of the family, falling apart. Weeping her heart out in Arthur's arms, harsh sobs wracking her body and railing at the sky. Bert taking one horrified look and walking out, straight to the pub where he had spent every single, silent, solitary night since the end of the war five years before. The image of his father, a generation removed but destroyed just the same, but destroyed by a different war. Reggie taking her arm and walking her firmly out of the door, not turning toward the local but steering her up the hill and away, just walking, not talking.

Fast. She had to scurry to keep up, and suddenly he looked down at her, noticed her plight and stopped abruptly, embarrassed by his lack of awareness and his lack of chivalry.

'I'm sorry, Millie,' he muttered, 'I just had to get out of there.'

She gave him a watery smile.

'I felt the same way,' she confessed, then to her chagrin, burst into tears, finally giving way to the flood of emotion she had done her best to hold back on this most terrible of days.

And suddenly she felt warm arms around her, Reggie enveloping her immediately in a bear hug, and for one long moment she leant her hot, sore face against his chest and surrendered to the comfort of his arms.

His heartbreakingly, almost familiar arms. In the next moment, pulling away, shocked, appalled that for an instant he had become Stanley for her, Stanley who was dead and gone. Stanley, who was irreplaceable.

He noticed her discomfiture and understood.

'I miss him too, Millie,' he said, awkwardly 'He was such a great kid, and he was so full of talent.'

Millie nodded, mutely, not trusting herself to speak.

'I'm lonely, Millie,' Reggie added, suddenly, in a rush, 'and I know you are too. Would you like to go for a walk with me at the weekend, or to the pictures or something?'

Millie stared at him for a moment, flustered and utterly taken aback. Then smiled gratefully at him.

'That would be lovely, Reggie. I'd like that.'

Unexpectedly feeling her spirits soaring and realising she meant it, with all her heart.

Part Eight

1952, Australia, Recovery

B ye Mum.'
May jumped as she heard the sound of the back door slamming, then rushing to the window, she smiled and waved cheerfully as she saw Irene swinging her way jauntily down the path to the road where her friends were waiting for her, a whole gaggle of them meeting up each day to walk the mile to school.

She leant against the window frame and watched for a long moment, relishing the bright morning sunshine and the way her daughter seemed to stride as she walked, her new-found confidence seeming to grow with each new day.

Australia had been kind to Irene, the sunshine and the limitless fresh food nourishing her like a sunflower turning towards the light.

The journey hadn't been kind to May though, she shuddered even now to remember the hours and days of desperate, endless sea sickness, curled up in the cramped little cabin, the dank air stale with the smell of vomit. They had travelled in a cabin shared between six women including Irene, Jimmy mercifully in the men's area and separated from them at night. He seemed to relish the movement of the ship, and each day, after reluctantly standing in the doorway and gingerly leaning in to see if May had improved at all, he would leave as soon as he decently could to stride the decks and breathe the sharp salt air.

Irene was also terribly sick for the first few days, the ship's pitching and rolling passage across the Bay of Biscay rendering most of its passengers insensible. She pulled through in time to see Gibraltar, however, and was entranced by the sunlight gleaming on the rock and the monkeys sitting chattering and watching as the cooped-up emigrants went ashore to find and stretch their land-legs again.

Out of the shadow of her father, she began to relax. And with her mother so sick and incapacitated, for the first time in her closeted life she began to discover a little of her own independence, running around the decks with new-found friends, playing deck tennis for hours, squealing with delight as the deck would tip and add an unexpected swoop and height to her leap. Learning to sneak into the forbidden areas, open only to the taciturn crew, being shouted out one day by an officer because she had ignored the command to stay inside during rough weather and was found clinging to the rail at the front of the ship, laughing wildly as the spray from the waves soaked her streaming face and hair.

Free for the first time from family, free from constraint and free from fear.

She was entranced by the sights and smells of exotic countries, especially when they stopped off in magical Ceylon where the warmth of the people who played with her curls and gave her exquisite fruit she tasted for the first time entranced her, finally helping her to forget the deprivation of the rations which had been part of her life since before she was born.

Then her first glimpse of Australia, the boat docking in Sydney to great fanfare and excitement, May finally up and about to be with her, clutching her hand tightly and staring as they docked for the first time in this strange, wild new land.

A blur of an interview for Jimmy, the three of them dispatched almost immediately on a train to Melbourne, the heat and discomfort of a third-class carriage telling bitterly on the little family, struggling to readjust to life at close quarters after six weeks on the ship. Jimmy tense and irritable but luckily too enthralled by the passing scenery to take it out on May or Irene who huddled quietly together, sliding back into their safe mode of not attracting attention to themselves, withdrawing into a collective, safe place.

Safe for now.

It had been good for a while, May reflected, resting her suddenly weary face against the window frame as she watched Irene scampering down the road with her friends. Suddenly she pulled herself up and leant out of the window, cupping her hands around her mouth.

'Irene!' she called. 'Not through the bush! And stick with the others!'

She grinned wryly when her daughter threw her a mock bow and ran off, shaking her mop of unruly curls as she did so. It was rather a lonely road back from school, and May liked Irene to walk with her friends rather than alone, but with her English-borne fear of spiders and snakes, she had also been expressly forbidden to 'run native' and come home cross-country, or through the bush, as they now called it.

May took a cloth and methodically began the daily task of

scrubbing at the creeping mould which was part of life up here in the tropics, allowing her mind to drift back to Melbourne and the beginning of their lives in Australia, but never once allowing herself to remember London and the family she could not begin to face she might never see again. Those she had loved with all her heart and then lost, if not to the war then to her husband and to all the choices she had felt compelled to make and the promises she believed she had to live with.

The hole that May left when she went felt like a physical, aching void to Lydia.

Each day, she awoke to a sickening, sinking realisation that her sister had gone, and this sense of being alone was oddly heightened by the bustle of the household around her, normal life continuing as if no one could see that she was drowning, sucked a little deeper each day into that dark pit from which she could see no escape.

Nobody except Arthur. Arthur knew, but he didn't know how to help her. He watched her silently across the divide growing, not so much between himself and his wife, but between Lydia and the rest of the world. As each day passed, she seemed to become a little more directionless, a little more listless. She no longer hummed to herself as she cooked. Her black curls grew matted and lank, he realised with a sudden pang that he could not remember when he'd last seen her brushing it out in long, sure strokes in front of her mirror as they made ready for bed, something which he'd always loved to watch as her reflection smiled back at him. His efforts to reach her felt increasingly futile, just a few weeks past she would respond to him, but lately he had felt her body stiffen in his arms, both rigid with despair as she slipped further and further away. Discreetly, he went to talk to the doctor who had looked after the family all their lives, and who had tended Lydia on the day that she had miscarried. He looked sympathetically at the thin young man sitting at his desk, the desperation he was feeling showing in the dark shadows under his eyes, and said grimly,

'In any other circumstance, I would tell you to get her pregnant as soon as you could, but you both already know that I doubt she'll ever be able to now. I'm so sorry.' Arthur bowed his head to hide the tears prickling in his eyes. He and Lydia had long since accepted that they couldn't have another child, but it felt so hard to hear it spelled out quite so baldly. 'What do you think we should do?'

The doctor sighed and looked down at his notepad, fiddling with a pen between his fingers and thumb. 'She's a strong girl. I think you just need to keep her as busy as you can, and hope that this will pass in time.'

But when Arthur came home from work the following night, he realised immediately that time was not healing, and that his wife's condition was deteriorating rapidly. The kitchen was dark and the fire in the stove had long since gone out. Bert was spending more and more time at the pub these days, and he remembered Reggie saying he was taking Millie out to the pictures tonight, and the house felt empty and cold.

It was then that he heard the sound, a sound that he had heard years before, a low, eerie keening sound that could only be coming from one person. Horrified, he took the stairs two and a time, then paused reluctantly for an infinitesimal moment by their door, afraid to open it onto what awaited him within. Steeling himself, he grasped the door knob and twisted it firmly. For a moment he couldn't see, struggling to adjust to the gloom of twilight in the unlit room, then his eyes made out a hunched figure crouched on the floor by the bed, clutching at something and rocking back and forth, back and forth, the unearthly sound whimpering and hissing between teeth clenched against unfathomable distress. In a few paces, he had reached her, put his hands on her thin shoulders and turned her to face him. The first thing he registered was the tiny nightgown she was clutching to her breast. One of Irene's, long since abandoned and outgrown, clutched now with the desperate fervour of a frantic and tortured soul. The second thing he registered was the blood. Bright red and oozing fatly from his wife's wrists, the jagged tears in sharp relief against the papery whiteness of her skin. The darker blood drying on the edges of the broken glass lying next to her where she knelt, discarded now as a means to an end.

In that moment, Arthur felt unutterably alone. Helpless in the face of his wife's despair for the second time in his life, he swept her up bodily into his shaking arms and carried her downstairs to the kitchen, praying that someone would come home soon to help him. Glancing around, he caught sight of the tea towel hanging over the edge of the sink. Settling Lydia down on the floor and leaning her back against a leg of the table, he began inexpertly to bind her unresisting wrists with strips of the cloth that he shredded with his teeth, acutely aware of Lydia's eyes locked mutely onto his own. He could not look at her. How could he look at her when he could not help her? A sob rising inexorably in his throat, he wrenched himself away from her anguished gaze, jumping with shock as the kitchen door opened suddenly behind him. To his shame, he couldn't contain the tears as Millie and Reg walked in. Horrorstruck but then briskly purposeful, they took control as Arthur finally fell apart. Called the doctor, talked to Lydia quietly and calmly while they waited for the ambulance to arrive. Made him tea while his wife, his Lydia, was manhandled into it and taken away to the place they'd all heard whispered about, the butt of many an unthinking and cruel joke. Bexley Mental Hospital. The lynchpin of the family and the love of his life.

His Lydia.

She was allowed no visitors.

Each day began the same, the doctors coming to talk to her about how she was feeling, the students staring curiously while she turned her face to the wall as the endless tears would begin to drip, culminating into rivulets running unheeded down her shuttered face.

What could she tell them? That her first hope had perished in a pool of blood on a privy floor? That the baby twin she had once mothered had died in the dust in Burma? That her sister, once her baby and now a grown woman whom, nonetheless, she felt instinctively needed her protection from the man she had unwittingly chosen, was now far out of her reach? That another child she felt had redeemed her, given her a new reason for living, was now a world away from her and that she was unlikely ever to set eyes on her ever again?

How could it possibly help to tell them this? What could these well-meaning, fresh-faced people in white coats possibly offer to ease this relentless pain? She spent hours at her allotted task. Her occupational therapy was deemed to be scrubbing sheets, a monotonous task designed to distract her mind from its distress and soothe her with its repetitive simplicity, while in actual fact the mindless chore simply allowed her more time to dwell on the past. Lydia didn't know how long she had been there or how long she would be required to stay. Her mind began to blur to the passage of time. Nothing seemed to penetrate through to her anymore, she felt as if she were groping her way through a thick pea-souper, all colours and sounds muted and distant.

Until the day she heard the screaming. Shrill, piercing and out of control, the screaming of a woman who had truly, completely, lost her mind. One moment, she had been scrubbing at the sheets, the next, she had seen three spots of blood against the coarse white cotton, the stark contrast flicking a switch darkly concealed in her memory. Then suddenly she heard the screaming, utterly unaware that the ungodly sound was emanating from her own mouth, gasping and panting for breath as the shutters slammed down hard in her mind to try and stop the pain and the loss of that desperate moment from sending her utterly insane. The chill of a needle slipping into her thigh, the blanket of oblivion sliding surely, blessedly, over her.

Her treatment regime changed. Dimly aware that she was being slid, like a slab of meat on the butcher's block, into a hammock-like contraption, then the bone-chilling shock of ice-water pouring over her naked, defenceless body. Over and over and over again. Then after another indiscriminate passage of time, feeling, but not understanding, that Arthur was there with her again, his arms around her as she tried to shrink away from harsh voices raised in bitter dispute. Arthur's voice telling her in a low, clear tone that there was another treatment that could be tried. That their family doctor had suggested it tentatively, that there had been success with it in some suicidal patients. Electroconvulsive therapy. A current to be arced through her agonised mind, a healing current to shock her out of her torment.

Arthur's iron composure finally cracked when Lydia raised her defeated eyes to meet his, lifted her scarred wrists up in supplication, and in a tiny, brittle voice so unlike the tough little London sparrow he had always known, begged for it to be done.

✧ ✧ ✧

Lydia was aware before she opened her eyes that today was different.

Today, the doctors were coming to decide if she was fit to be discharged, ready to go home. She stretched her legs experimentally under the coarse sheet and winced as every muscle threatened to spasm against her movement, she had endured no less than ten ECT treatments and each one had left her battered and bruised, four nurses restraining her arms and legs during the sessions such that she could not break her own bones through the involuntary flailing of her limbs. She had, in fact, dislocated her left shoulder on one occasion, but that, she reflected grimly, bore no resemblance to the pain she had been enduring in her mind. Her mental state had improved dramatically from the very first session, after which she had found a quiet peace in her new allotted task of knitting blankets, despite struggling a little with the blunt needles they had provided for her. Needle through, wool around, needle off. Needle through, wool around, needle off. Nothing else mattered. After the next session, the knitting made her think of May, and she smiled ruefully as she looked at her handiwork, comparing it mentally with what her talented sister would have produced in a fraction of the time it had taken her to knit a single square. Gradually she became aware of a new sensation, and sat enjoying the uniqueness of what she was experiencing. She was thinking about May, and she was smiling. After a few more sessions, she asked for pen and paper and began to write. She wrote prodigiously, to May, to Arthur, to Millie. She tried to write to Reg and Bert too, but found that reminded her too much of war letters and turned her thoughts away from memories she did not yet feel ready to face. She wrote poems, she wrote sentences and phrases, anything which seemed to her to encapsulate and ex-

172

press the feelings she had bottled up for so long. The loss of her mother now seemed something she could grieve for, rather than rail against, and while this made her weep as she wrote of it, the tears were the gentle tears of sadness rather than the bitter ones of regret. She climbed gingerly out of bed and sat quietly, looking around the tiny, pale green cell that had been her home for nearly four long months. Home. The thought of her warm, welcoming kitchen made her heart lurch with sudden desperate yearning, and determinedly she got up and began to stack up her precious note books and fold her few possessions neatly into the bag that Arthur had brought for her, willing the doctors to come soon to sanction her release from this place which she hated with all her heart, at the same time as knowing she owed it her very life.

Some weeks later, Arthur came home from work a little earlier than usual, enjoying the warmth in the evening air but in all honesty, increasingly trepidatious as he approached the house. He could never allow himself to relax, not since the day that he had discovered that his wife wanted to die. Much as he had tried to understand her plight, he couldn't help but see her need to escape her reality as a reflection on him as a husband. That without giving her a child, he alone was not enough for her to want to live. He let himself in quietly through the kitchen door, then stood stock still, transfixed in wonderment. Lydia turned to him from her place at the kitchen sink, raising puzzled eyes to meet his.

'Hello love, what's wrong?' she asked, alarmed and bewildered by his trancelike pose.

Arthur swallowed hard. 'You're humming, love,' he replied softly. 'You're humming under your breath while you're cooking.' He wiped tears starting from the corners of his eyes and took her in his arms. 'The music's come home.'

At first, Jimmy had revelled in his new life, discovering a free-dom in Melbourne he had never experienced before, work-ing in a garage servicing huge trucks and gigantic farm machinery, the likes of which England had never seen. Everything bigger, and more space than he could have dreamed of, as beautiful as the wild mountains of Italy that he had seen in the war, but without the constraints of discipline and the endless, numbing fear that had shredded his nerves during those relentlessly brutal years.

May and Irene relaxed a little, almost daring to believe that life could be better, that the New World would also be new and fresh and shiny for the likes of themselves.

But not for long.

One day, someone played a joke on Jimmy, pushed it a little too far. Frayed tempers snapping, a hard-thrown punch, a broken jaw; Jimmy fired and the family dropped from the New Australian Programme.

Nowhere to go.

Until a mate gave him a recommendation, a nod to another friend. The next thing May knew, she was packing up their little house and they were on the train again, this time heading to Bris-bane, the tropics and sugar cane country. To her utter, heartfelt relief, Jimmy got the job, servicing and keeping the huge hydrau-lic cane cutters working night and day. He adapted to the heat and humidity like he was born to it, and Irene seemed to cope too, but not May.

She spent the first few weeks prostrate with Dengue fever, then struggled to endure the endless damp, pushing her clinging hair back from her forehead with shaking hands as she mopped down the mould from the walls of their cramped cabin, a task she needed to repeat almost daily to stay on top of the creeping, stinking mildew. The spiders and snakes terrified her, the climate exhausted her. Her only consolation was that Irene seemed happier than ever at her new school, and Jimmy was rarely at home, the long hours finally bringing him the money he so craved, allowing them to move into a more airy house before the year was out.

She allowed herself a smile again as she looked around her. The house was now as under control as it ever could be in this climate, aired and scrubbed and gleaming bright, so bright compared to the cosy warmth of the long-distant kitchen light she still held so close to her heart.

He seemed so much happier than she had ever remembered him, the physical work and the easy-going nature of his new mates channelling his restless energy into something positive rather than allowing him to travel his usual destructive path.

She shuddered suddenly, remembering when they had last gone out with his mates, a date, almost like when they used to go dancing up in the bright lights of the London West End.

They had been invited to a dance in the local social club, and the two of them had found some of their old joy whirling around the floor to the beat of the music and applause. A sound that they had forgotten making their feet light as feathers and their laughter ring out, an accordion, playing cheerful ditties then lapsing into slow folksongs to close the hot but happy night. Jimmy talking to the band, asking about the accordion, then much to May's astonishment, buying his own and beginning to take lessons.

She winced painfully as she remembered those lessons. Jimmy, scowling furiously at his music as he tried to decipher the chords, painstakingly and painfully making progress. Slow progress. Then frustration kicking in, the accordion thrown down, a slammed door. Returning from the pub and reaching for his belt to take his rage out on May.

And then that incredible day, when she had been alone, quietly working her way through the housework, her eyes noting the dust gathering on the abandoned instrument. Picking it up and feeling its weight, experimenting a little and stopping short with guilty pleasure as the rich sound rang out. Settling herself on the edge of the table and peering at the discarded music, running Jimmy's lessons over in her mind, finding her fingers suddenly dancing across the keys. Music swelling out, a gift she had never known she possessed.

May pressed her hand to her heart as she let her mind wander back to those days, days when she would start to do her chores but would allow herself to be distracted earlier and earlier to practise, her expertise growing ever faster. Losing herself in the sound that swelled forth from her increasingly skilled fingers, the sounds of the melodies she had grown up with in London filling the house and her heart with joy.

Losing herself in the music.

Not hearing the door open, not hearing Jimmy coming home. Not seeing the jealous rage etched across his face, at least not until the first blow had caught her and sent her sprawling, the accordion falling from her senseless hands to the floor, where he stamped on it until the mechanism was utterly destroyed and he could turn back to beat his wife.

That had been the first time he had really hurt her, she acknowledged grimly to herself, unconsciously rubbing at her wrist, the bone had broken at such a difficult angle that they had had trouble resetting it and warned her it would never be quite the same again, that she had better be 'more careful on the stairs' in future.

And it never was the same again. The accordion gone, the house, her soul and her daughter bereft of music.

He warned her never to play again.

⬦ ⬦ ⬦

Later that day, Irene swung out of the school gates, her bag slung casually over her shoulder while she chatted to her friends. The sun was relentless today, and the five girls panted as they walked down the long road, then with one accord they stopped in the shade of a tree at the bottom of the hill which led back to where they all lived. It was a dusty road with very little shade, and suddenly Jean, one of the oldest of the group, grinned around at them all, her hands resting on her hips and her eyes flashing a challenge.

'Let's cut through the bush,' she suggested, 'it's just as steep but at least it's shady!'

All the girls hesitated momentarily, like Irene, they had all been told not to do this, but the deep shade of the gum trees looked so much more appealing than the dry dust of the steep track winding up and away from them in the searing heat of the afternoon, the light shimmering from the hot, cracked paving.

Suddenly the decision was made, and the girls, complicit in their daring, ran together into the enticing cool of the bush, their voices ringing out with collective bravery. Collective bar one, the one they had unwittingly left behind.

Irene, frozen in an agony of indecision, glancing anxiously up the lonely track then with trepidation into the bush, afraid to be left behind but equally afraid to follow.

And then, she probably made the worst decision she could have made, a decision no Australian-born child would ever have made. Biting her lip, she clutched her bag to her chest and ran, ran as fast as she could into the forbidden bush alone to try and catch up with her friends, their voices tempting her and encouraging her onwards as they ran on, out of sight ahead of her.

All of a sudden, Irene stopped short. Accustomed as she was

becoming to her beloved Australia, her London eyes could scarcely process what she was seeing before her.

A tiny clearing in the undergrowth. The heat lying so heavily in the air that she could see it shimmering in front of her, shimmering like a mirage. And in that deadly mirage, a snake, bigger than she could have ever have imagined. Enormous, alien, silent. And looking down at her.

Irene froze again, transfixed with horror by the huge, patterned head, completely still and poised above her own. Slowly, oh so slowly, she allowed her eyes to travel down its gently swaying body to see the thick, glistening coils piled in a sinuous heap on the ground, feeling her breath labouring in her throat as she struggled to suck in the glutinous air.

Irene couldn't move, and it was probably that immobility that saved her life from the carpet snake she had unwittingly surprised. In any event, she was never able to remember what happened next, a complete, merciful blank until the moment when she arrived, soaked in sweat and tears to run into her mother's horrified, uncomprehending arms. Unable to talk, her voice locked down deep inside her, the fear of those cold, beady eyes rendering her speechless and incapable for the next two days. An unreachable silence that her father finally beat out of her when he lost his temper the second night, demanding that the shocked child tell them what had happened, then beating her until she finally opened her mouth to scream out the terrible story, her mother rocking back and forth as Jimmy beat her again and again for walking alone into the bush. Wrapping her arms around her afterwards but always too late, not moving to intercept nor stop the blows, as ever, making herself as inconspicuous as possible until Jimmy's rage was spent.

Spent on their traumatised, defenceless, twelve-year-old daughter.

✧ ✧ ✧

Millie and Reggie were married in a quiet but beautiful ceremony the following spring after May, Lydia and Jimmy had left.

Lydia stood clutching Arthur's hand with tears rolling down her cheeks as she watched. Remembering Millie marrying her baby brother a lifetime ago, and now mercifully finding joy with the elder. Millie's face solemn but radiant, Reggie so choked with emotion that Bert, his best man, had to hand him a handkerchief half way through his vows.

Their courtship had been tentative and shy, neither wanting to presume, neither wanting to risk disturbing their carefully rebuilt lives, underpinned by a dark, pervasive grief that both had worked so hard to bury.

Yet both hopeful, their war spirit lending them a certain indomitable optimism, finally learning to trust one another and to believe that they could enjoy a shared happiness together. Already knowing and comfortable with each other, a wealth of shared memories, both utterly cognisant of what the other had endured during the war years and in its bitter aftermath. Millie had shown Reggie some of Stanley's drawings, and he had wept with her when he saw the graphic depiction of Dunkirk, until that moment the memory still buried, raw and unexplored in his mind. And laughed and kissed her when she shyly, doubtfully, showed him that other picture, that had been so personal between her and his brother, but now could once again be a shared pleasure.

The joy and mutual relief that they had found each other, the only other person who could truly understand them, their past, their ever present grief, their hope for a future.

Two people, who, when their son was born, knew that he would be named Stanley to commemorate a lost brother and a lost husband, without needing words, explanation nor justification.

Just a simple joy that a shared pain could become a blossoming love and a poignant new beginning for one little family finding its feet, reinventing themselves and learning to survive in this strange new world.

Moving forward together.

When May received the letter from Millie, with the scribbled, jaunty note added on the bottom from her eldest brother Reggie, she sank down at the kitchen table and wept with the desolation of the unhomed. Pictures of the house on Muswell Hill swam through her mind, memories of bringing up baby Irene mingling with her imaginary images of the new baby, Stanley, whom she could clearly visualise from Millie's vivid description of a child she felt she already knew.

Her twin's namesake and a child she was unlikely to ever meet, born half a world and a life away. While her own daughter lay upstairs in her darkened bedroom, recovering from the horror of the snake in the bush and the beating that had brought that knowledge to light. Once again too bruised and battered to be sent to school in the aftermath of her father's unfettered rage.

May covered her face in shame and wept until her tears were spent.

When Irene finally limped warily downstairs later that day, driven by hunger and an unspeakable loneliness, she was struck by the silence that greeted her, eyes flitting warily around, searching for a sign that her father was home. She paused uncertainly in the kitchen doorway regarding her mother with anxious eyes as she sat, motionless in the half light of the early evening, a letter opened before her on the scratched surface of the breakfast table. Memories of another day, her mother weeping on her knees holding an inconsolable Millie, rising unbidden and unwanted in her mind.

She shook her head painfully and went forward to touch her mother's slender shoulder, felt a faint quiver emanating from the taut muscles under her fingers.

'Mum?' she asked quietly, not wanting to scare her, but nonetheless May jumped like a frightened kitten. But the visage that she turned to Irene in the next instant was anything but submissive, and Irene recoiled instinctively, shocked at the rage and determination she could see vying for superiority on her mother's face.

'What is it, whatever's happened?' she whispered, appalled, and May visibly collected herself to focus on her daughter, standing confused and fearful before her.

'I want to go back.' The words sounded guttural and harsh as she uttered them, drawn from her dry throat exhausted with hours of weeping and lonely soul-searching.

Soul-searching that was long overdue. The beatings, the enforced submission and weakening of her will. The dehumanisation and the stripping of her basic maternal instinct now rising like bile in her throat and making her gag with unexpected vitriol, bubbling unchecked from depths she had never known she possessed. The face of her beloved but betrayed daughter, the daughter she could have lost, be it to bombs, beatings, or the trials and tribulations of a country they had tried to adopt but that remained utterly foreign at the core despite their best efforts to fit in.

'I want to go home, Irene. I won't force you, you can stay here with your father if you want, but please come, darling, please come with me. I'm going back to London, I want us to go home. Both of us.'

And Irene could never be prouder, nor would ever forget the moment when May told Jimmy. Not just that they were leaving Australia to return to London, but that they were going home without him. That May was leaving him.

And when Jimmy fell to his knees and begged, declaring his love for them, finally the storm broke. The storm that had been brewing within May since the first time he had raised his hand to her when she was only nineteen, a storm that had simmered and seethed darkly since she had chosen to give up the love of a kind and gentle man to do her duty to this soldier, this returning war hero, this violent and vicious man she called husband and father to her child. May swept to her feet like a vengeful angel, years of suppressed emotion lending her wings to fly.

Vindicated and full of joy, mother and daughter flew.

Part Nine

Journey's End

The vast ship towered above the harbour walls in Sidney, dwarfing the friends and relatives crowding like tiny, insignificant ants on the dockside to say goodbye. Already half forgotten, left behind in the hearts of those whose thoughts had already turned to a different life a world away from here.

May and Irene had returned the way they came, crammed into a crowded carriage of a hot and dusty train. A similar journey, perhaps, but with oh such different emotions clutched within their breasts.

Twelve-year-old Irene, a wiser and more self-sufficient girl than the ten-year-old child who had once travelled out on a similar ship, tasting independence and freedom for the first time. A young woman who had already learned at such cost not to trust her father, nor indeed to rely wholly on her mother. Sadder but wiser, and ready, oh so ready for the new challenges ahead of her.

She smiled broadly as she turned to her mother, leaning out on the rail, streamer in hand ready to throw into the throng of people waving valiantly from the quay. May looked radiant, her black curls blowing loose and free about her tanned, smiling face, the happiness and peace she had found in her decision reflecting in every nuance of her expression.

Then in the space of a heartbeat, she froze.

Irene saw her stiffen, her lips pressed tight and her face paling under her tan. Then Irene heard it too, her heart turning to ice and her knees to jelly as she heard the howl of a berserker, a man who had terrified her and hurt her such that her only happy and secure memories were the nights of the Blitz, happier in an air raid shelter snug within the love of her family than with this mad-man she called her father.

'May!' Jimmy stood on the dockside with his head tilted back, the end of May's bright streamer suddenly, inexplicably, caught deftly in his hand. Tears were running unchecked down his rav-aged face and people turned to stare, this unrestrained emotion suddenly shocking and raw in the harsh glare of the midday sun.

And May faltered.

Irene felt the rage blistering within her then, that her mother could be broken like this again, that this man could thwart their plans and determine their fates yet again with a single word. This man who had returned from battle to bring violence into their lives instead of completing their family, and destroying the peace that she had known as a child in a London brought close to its knees by years of war.

'Mum.' She spoke urgently, her low tone unwittingly echo-ing May's own words when she had asked Irene to return home with her. 'Mum, he will never, never change, Mum, please look away. Please come away, Mum. Come with me.' Her desperation at these unbearable stakes making her voice waver with those last words, and with the iron discipline she had learned at her mother's knee, she bit down hard on her lip, forcing herself to calm down to allow her mother to rally her thoughts.

'May!' Jimmy howled again, dropping to his knees, the very vision of a man whose courage had long since evaporated along with his pride. Dramatically, he flung open a case he had been clutching, a new accordion gleaming incongruously, garish in the bright sunlight, 'for you, May! I bought it for you!'

And May laughed harshly at that. Abruptly, she became aware of another voice, dearly beloved, a low, insistent voice cutting across the edge of her consciousness. And finally, her maternal conscience.

She turned away from the pitiful, desperate scene below and looked deeply, repentantly into Irene's eyes.

'Let's go, love.' She took one last, scornful look at the wretched figure on the quay below and raised her hand as if to wave, Jimmy scrambling to his feet suddenly in a drunken ecstasy of pathetic hope. Then her slim arm described a graceful arc as she hurled the streamer she had been holding in her hand.

And turned firmly and joyously to hug her daughter, Irene suddenly trembling, laughing and weeping with shock and delight at her mother's decisive and unutterably symbolic action. Both women leaving the rail to explore their new floating home without so much as a backward glance at the broken man below clutching a torn streamer, fluttering endlessly and pointlessly in the sudden breeze.

Lydia counted down the days, knowing that she could only truly guess at when her sister and niece might return, the times of the ship, imprecise and approximate, riling her nerves.

She could not sleep. Arthur worried at her agitation, and spent long hours talking to her into the night as he held her in his ever-patient arms. The thought of seeing the sister she had brought up and the niece she had mothered causing her to relive those agonising days after she lost their child, the loss which had been assuaged to a degree by loving Irene, but suffered anew when Jimmy had taken them away.

Little Stanley partly helped and partly confused her emotions, the very image of both May and Irene as babies, Millie and Reggie serene in their new-found contentment.

She found herself contemplating the scrubbed floorboards in the kitchen one afternoon, seeing but not seeing those bright splashes of blood that had signified the end of one tiny life. She became aware of Arthur's ever-anxious eyes watching her, but also began to become aware of a sadness without a sense of bitterness, a loss without tragedy. A certain acceptance of an event that she had never previously been able to rationalise nor let go. Lydia had gradually and finally understood, and now recognised deep in her heart, that she was born to mother each and every one of them. The days when she had lost her own mother and then her child were the days she became surrogate to the family, her siblings, both younger and older, learning to depend on her, then the next generation in turn. And for the first time, Lydia felt pride swelling in her heart that she had taken on such a difficult role at such a young age, and that she had helped them all pull through these years which had tested their family so ruthlessly just as they had challenged the very survival of Europe and the world.

As the weeks went by, postcards began to arrive, tattered yet somehow full of the warmth of the countries they depicted. Bit by bit, Lydia began to track the ship's progress around the globe,

Ceylon, Cairo, Gibraltar, a calmness finally descending upon her as the inevitability of the family's impending reunion came closer.

She awoke one morning, suddenly aware that she had slept long and deeply for the first time in as long as she could remember. She opened her eyes peaceably to find Arthur smiling at her, his eyes lit by some secret knowledge.

'Good morning, sweetheart,' he said, quietly. 'There's a train due in soon. I think it's time we went for a walk.'

The silvery light of a wintry sun shining on the wet platform held May's eyes for a long moment as the train drew into the station, she and Irene both shivering convulsively in London's winter chill after the long Australian summer. Both stunned by the onslaught of memories the train journey evoked as it rattled towards Muswell Hill, the sights and sounds of the awakening city calling to them like some half-forgotten but intimately treasured dream.

As the train drew to a halt, May stepped down briskly, then turned back to help Irene who was numb with fatigue and drained by the very anticipation of this moment.

Another woman watched incredulously from a distance, steadied by the arm of the man whom she knew loved her with all his heart. Joyously noting the new decisiveness, the plucky independence of the other woman's demeanour as she called for a porter, reached for her daughter with a firm hand, and turned to gaze straight into her eyes across the long stretch of platform between them.

'Hello Lydia,' May said, simply. 'I'm home.'

And at that moment, laughing and crying, Irene flung herself at Arthur with the simple innocence of the child he had always loved despite the two long years past, and he swept her up into his arms and swung her around in joy.

And turned to watch the two sisters leaving the platform quietly, arm in arm. The walking wounded of two world wars, and survivors of their own more personal but equally devastating conflicts.

Walking wounded perhaps, but as they leaned towards each other now in a new but sweet harmony, neither one was limping.

The End

MAY 2014

Lightning Source UK Ltd.
Milton Keynes UK
UKOW06f0041250916

283742UK00002B/6/P